The Mice that Roared

A Disarming Adventure

--- with hope for the future,

Tom

T. F. HECK

An Insights Consulting Production

Copyright © 2016 Thomas F. Heck

Contact the author at insights@aya.yale.edu

ISBN: 1533437157
ISBN-13: 978-1533437150

CONTENTS

CHAPTER 1

DANCING ON DECK

Now is the month of Maying,
When merry lads are playing.
They may dance like heck
On the afterdeck,
But how long will they be staying?

The Permanent Joint Headquarters at Northwood, near London, is no Pentagon. But in its unimpressive suburban way it fulfills many of the latter's command functions for the British armed forces. It resembles a campus more than a building; it is said to have extensive underground bunkers that can withstand a nuclear attack.

Northwood Headquarters—as it is known—monitors in a general way where Britain's strategic ballistic-missile submarines are deployed, with due regard for stealth. Two-way communications are infrequent. Such submarines do not typically reveal their whereabouts through outgoing messages, but they do have ways of "phoning home" from time to time to update Headquarters as to their status. Of course, they can receive nuclear missile launch orders at any time.

On a deployment that began in late April, SSBN *Vengeance*, one of the four Trident missile submarines in the British fleet, has been much quieter than usual. "Uncommunicative to a fault" might be a fair way of describing her messaging behavior, especially in a time of relatively low international tension. Concern has arisen at Northwood as to her exact whereabouts. The most recent coded messages to her having gone unanswered, the Commander-in-Chief Fleet (CINCFLEET) staff is wondering whether a communications malfunction or perhaps something more serious has occurred.

The silence of the *Vengeance* is about to be broken, but not in ways anticipated by the Royal Navy.

10:45 GMT on a sunny Wednesday morning in May 2019

Imagine the surprise of Cmdr. Rogers, the Northwood Duty Officer on this particular morning shift, as a totally unexpected flashing icon appears on the large electronic map of the British Isles in the Situation Room. It is clear that the transponder of the *Vengeance* has just been turned on, and is blatantly disclosing to Headquarters and everyone else her precise location—not in the North Atlantic, where she was expected, but off the *south* coast of England, cruising very close to shore.

"I'll be damned!" exclaims Rogers. "That's the *Vengeance* flashing on screen! What in bloody hell is she doing down there? Has McGinty lost his marbles?"

Another officer in the darkened room exclaims, in a similarly exasperated way, "She has not responded to our radio transmissions for nearly three weeks! We don't know if there's a mutiny or hijacking in progress, or what!"

"Could there have been a mechanical failure? An electronics malfunction?" another voice asks.

The display shows the submarine to be slowly approaching Brighton, the popular seaside resort south of London. The

Vengeance continues to ignore all radio communications from Headquarters.

Rogers quickly orders the RAF liaison officer on duty to scramble an interceptor jet from an available southern-sector RAF station to reconnoiter SSBN *Vengeance* off Brighton and report. Turning to his adjutant, he asks, "What Royal Navy assets do we have in the vicinity? Any helicopters?"

"Sir," he replies, "the Prince of Wales, an amphibious commando ship that launches helicopters, is off Eastbourne, about 50 km. east of Brighton."

"Request that it dispatch a helicopter with marines a.s.a.p. for a contingency boarding," orders Rogers. "Alert the other Navy ships in the area to approach the *Vengeance* with caution and report."

"Aye, aye, sir!"

A few minutes later, from a console in another part of the situation room, a radioman reports. "Sir, we have a report incoming from a Harrier. I'll switch it to the loudspeaker."

The RAF pilot's voice comes crackling across. "Tiger one-seven-two here. I have visual contact with the submarine. About thirty or forty crew members appear to be dancing on deck, waving white handkerchiefs... It looks like a line dance of some sort, and... the crew all seem to be in their skivvies! Flags are flying, including a large one from the sub's tower with a peace symbol. A small-boat escort has surrounded the sub. People are waving and cheering. Will continue to overfly. Tiger one-seven-two out."

"If a fleet of small craft is gathering around the sub," Rogers mutters. "It's going to be on the news, not to mention YouTube, in no time." He grabs a remote and brings up the volume on a BBC-TV news monitor, just as a scrolling headline appears on screen: NUCLEAR MISSILE SUB SURFACES NEAR BRIGHTON.

The BBC news anchor reports with measured urgency:

We interrupt this program for a breaking news bulletin. A British strategic nuclear-missile submarine has unexpectedly surfaced off the south coast of England. She is slowly cruising east between Shoreham Beach and Brighton with all flags flying. The crew, said to be wearing "the briefest of briefs," are reported to be doing a line-dance routine on deck whilst waving white handkerchiefs. A peace flag is flying. The Royal Navy thus far has no comment on why the sub is there or what she is doing. An interceptor jet has been seen flying low over the area. Stay tuned for more on this unfolding story. News media are rushing to the scene.

"Oh God!" exclaims Rogers. "It looks like the media are already picking up on this. Time to alert Admiral Hodgson." He reaches for a phone.

Wednesday morning, 11:00 GMT.

At about 11:00 AM, Leslie Prim, a fresh-faced reporter for the local BBC-TV station in Brighton, reaches the waterfront. She is preparing to cover the story live. The submarine has barely come into view to the southwest.

Her cameraman, Josh, zooms in on the sub and remarks, "Leslie, it looks like there's some kind of peace demonstration taking place on that sub's rear deck. I'd say they're line-dancing, wearing next to nothing. See the flags? Look!"

Leslie looks in the viewfinder. "Holy crap!" Just then her mobile phone rings. "Damn! Who could that be?" She switches on the phone. "Hello!"

"Hello, Ms. Prim?" The male voice was not familiar.

"Speaking."

"This is Commander McGinty aboard the SSBN *Vengeance*, the Trident missile submarine you may be able to see in the distance if you're on the Brighton waterfront."

"Yes, Commander McGinty, I'm right on the Brighton Esplanade and I can see your sub from here. Hold just a second please."

Leslie's mobile phone picks up the strains of the "Liberty Bell" march by Sousa—the opening theme music for Monty Python's Flying Circus—in the background. She puts it in speaker mode, holds her microphone close to it, and gestures to Josh to get this on tape.

Josh signals that he is now recording the conversation, and relaying it back to the station.

"We're on the air now. How did you reach me, Commander?"

"I telephoned your station on my mobile phone to speak with a BBC-TV reporter, and they put me through to you on your personal mobile. I agreed to be interviewed and to be recorded. My officers and crew thought that the media would like to know straight from us why we're cruising slowly along the south coast of England, making such a spectacle of ourselves."

"Yes, people are wondering, Commander. From here it looks like your crew is holding a choreographed peace demonstration of some sort on deck. Can you tell us what's happening? Has there been some kind of hijacking or mutiny?"

"Negative. This is *not* a mutiny or hijacking, and our communications systems are working fine. What you are witnessing is a collective action by the officers and crew of the *Vengeance* to take this sub and her nuclear missiles off-line, out of commission, for the good of humanity.

It has finally dawned on us—as officers and crew, but above all as human beings—that nuclear warfare is illegal, immoral, and unnecessary. We've decided we want no part of it. And we intend to draw attention to our message by surfacing from time to time and communicating with our fellow citizens in this way."

Prim's tone turns serious. "What kind of demands are you making, if any, Commander?"

"No demands—only a request. By going public with our dissent, we hope to start a genuine reversal of the nuclear arms race. We want Britain to lead a worldwide disarmament process, and we've decided to kick-start the process. I guess you could say we're trying to be the first nuclear domino to fall... and we hope that, with our nudge, all the rest will topple, too."

"Commander... are you saying that the entire crew and officers are with you on this?"

"Affirmative. It might be more accurate to say that I'm with them. We set nine dissenters ashore earlier today, with no hard feelings; the rest of our crew— about 120 sailors—are hanging together on this action."

Prim whispers to Josh, "Get a tighter shot of the sub!" As a close-up of the conning tower comes into view on the monitor, Prim resumes the interview.

"We've got a close-up of your submarine now, Commander. Is that name hanging on the conning tower, *Domino*, a reference to what you said about dominos toppling? Or is there another, perhaps theological, overtone?"

"You can take it either way, Ms. Prim. We think that the *Domino*, as a name, says more clearly what we're up to than the *Vengeance*. Don't you agree?"

"It does sound a lot less menacing," Prim remarks in a controlled tone of voice. "Have you already rechristened your sub with its new name, Commander?"

"Affirmative. All we're missing is the Champagne... and that may yet come!"

"You seem to be attracting quite an escort of small craft."

"The more the merrier! They help keep the wolves away."

"Can you give the listeners more detail on how you and your crew reached this decision? Was there some kind of debate and vote? Or did someone put some powder in your chowder, so to speak?"

"Actually, it was a long process. We were quietly submerged in the North Atlantic last month, armed and operational. While on station, my officers and crew had lots of opportunity to discuss honestly what we would do or not do, realistically, if a firm order to arm and launch missiles were ever received. Normally discussions like this just don't happen openly on a nuclear missile sub. We all quietly do our jobs. We compartmentalize, and we don't talk about the horrendous consequences of launching these missiles. We work our shifts, collect our paychecks, and hope and pray that the launch order doesn't come on our watch."

"So... did your crew just up one day and revolt?"

"No... it wasn't anything like that. All I can tell you is that over a period of weeks we experienced a collective change of heart. A consensus formed among the crew and officers that there was no way we were going to launch these damnable American doomsday weapons against anyone, either as a first strike or in some kind of over-the-top retaliation... In all honesty, none of us wanted to be involved in mass murder. None of us wants to engage in anti-population warfare, or even to threaten such a thing. It was a small, but significant, step from having that realization to deciding to take a public stand. That's what we're doing now, in case you haven't noticed."

"But aren't you directly disobeying orders? Couldn't you all be court-martialed?"

"Of course we could. 'No good deed goes unpunished.' We expect to lose our jobs and pensions and then some. But at least we're going to speak up—we're going to make our point and be reckoned with—before we surrender."

"So you're saying there's more at stake here than your individual jobs."

"Exactly! We're taking a public stand on the morality and legality of nuclear warfare. And we're starting today."

"But you could all be sent away for years or worse. Isn't this mutiny?"

"Look... any order we would receive to launch nuclear missiles would be illegal under *any* rules of war, because we would be killing huge numbers of civilians. Even *one* nuclear warhead, depending on the fallout it produced, could have unimaginable consequences for generations to come. We've got sixteen Trident missiles on this sub, each with three warheads—all of them much larger than what obliterated Hiroshima. Even launching *one* Trident missile would be an act of genocide! We don't want the blood of tens of thousands on our hands. It's not fair, it's not civil—it's just not British to expect us to do so."

"You're coming through loud and clear, Commander. Go on!"

"So we're just saying that we all have to back off from this kind of insanity. And we on the *Vengeance*—or the *Domino*, if you will—believe we have a rather unique means of getting the world's attention. We have a very powerful soap box. So we hope to continue doing exactly what we're doing now: threatening no one and talking sense to everyone, until the tide turns."

Prim motions to Josh to stop recording.

"Commander... is there a chance we could join you to continue this interview? Could we come aboard?"

"If you can find some kind of speedboat and come out and meet us, that might work. But you'd better hurry, because we are starting to attract the attention of the Royal Navy. They are sending escorts out our way who seem interested in doing more than just interviewing us."

Leslie and Josh begin to race toward Brighton Marina, intending to arrange for a zodiac-style speedboat to take them to the submarine.

CHAPTER 2

LESLIE BY A WHALE SWALLOWED

Unlike Jonah, who had to be thrown
By his mates into waters unknown,
This courageous female
Made a leap toward the whale;
Would she later her impulse bemoan?

Wednesday morning, 11:45 GMT.

Marshall Strong, Secretary of State for Defence, is in his office at Northwood awaiting the arrival of Admiral Roger Rakewell, First Sea Lord. As Rakewell walks in, Strong stands, glaring at him in disbelief.

"Rakewell, what in bloody hell has been going on with the *Vengeance* and her crew?"

Saluting as he enters, Rakewell replies, "Sir, as you have already been briefed, the *Vengeance* has not responded to any communications in the last three weeks. That's unusual, but not unheard of, since our missile subs can elect to maintain radio silence."

"But popping up off the coast of Brighton and holding a peace demonstration on deck. What's that all about?" Strong asks.

"My staff are watching the situation carefully, sir," replies Rakewell. "A BBC reporter has apparently been in direct contact by mobile phone with the Commander, Duff McGinty—one of our most reliable and experienced officers. If you switch on a telly, we might pick up a current report."

"Do you see a telly in this office?" glares Strong. "Listen, Rakewell, I want direct *military* communications restored with that sub by whatever means it takes. I don't care if you have to send a cutter out with a blasted megaphone. Order McGinty and his officers to stand down at once. If they don't, then relieve McGinty of command and send another senior officer aboard to restore command and control."

Rakewell, sensing that this is no time to discuss options, simply replies, "Aye-aye, sir!" and turns to exit. As he is walking out, he hears his boss bark, "And Rakewell... don't go far! Use our secure phone to issue your orders. The Prime Minister may want to see us both sooner rather than later."

Wednesday noon, 12:00 GMT.

As noon approaches, the submarine finds herself surrounded by an ever-growing flotilla of private vessels—dozens of them, their owners and passengers waving and cheering. They seem to know just what's going on, and they are very excited about it.

The crew dancing on deck is repeating its routines, to the tunes of *Liberty Bell* and *The Colonel Bogey March,* with ever greater panache. The music is coming from a loudspeaker aimed at the afterdeck. The encircling audience claps and urges them on. Some of the young women blow kisses and flash the handsome young sailors, as if to say "Look what you've been missing! Keep it up, guys!" The whole scene is getting noisy, with horns tooting, bells ringing, and now helicopters circling overhead.

Just as a Royal Navy frigate starts closing in from the sub's starboard side, a rapidly approaching zodiac skids onto the sub's port flank, and out jump two passengers—Leslie Prim and Josh, her cameraman. Sailors help them aboard and shove the zodiac off. Prim and Josh scamper inside a hatch as the crew clears the decks, preparing to dive.

Suddenly a helicopter from the Royal Marines swings into position directly above the sub's tower, sending spray flying in all directions. Its loudspeaker orders the sub to heave to. The sub holds its course as its hatches are made fast.

The chopper drops rappelling lines as it attempts to lower Marines to recover control of the *Vengeance*. But they can't secure a footing anywhere, because the submarine's deck is already awash. Several marines get soaked before the chopper hauls them back to safety.

The flotilla of small boats fans out in the ensuing confusion. Some of the boaters appear to be running interference for the sub, as they crisscross in front of the Royal Navy cutter, honking their horns and hampering its efforts to pursue the *Domino*.

Wednesday afternoon, 13:45 GMT.

After about an hour of evasive maneuvers, the *Domino* levels off, deep in the English Channel. The atmosphere aboard has become quiet and businesslike. The sailors who were dancing on deck have long since climbed back into their standard issue nylon overalls and returned to their posts.

Prim and Josh, having been led to a small wardroom, are preparing to interview Commander Duff McGinty and Executive Officer Richard Hartwell. Josh signals to Leslie that his video setup is ready.

Prim begins, "This is Leslie Prim, reporting from aboard the Trident nuclear missile submarine *Vengeance*, renamed the *Domino* by its crew. It is Wednesday afternoon at about 14:00 hours. With me is Commander Duff McGinty, the skipper of this formidable weapons system. He and his crew ceased responding to radio communications from the Royal Navy about three weeks ago, and are now on a surprise mission to advocate in a remarkably public way for nuclear disarmament. Commander, tell us in your own words what is happening. Is it accurate to call this action a hijacking?"

"We want the British authorities and the world to know that we are certainly *not* hijacking anything. This is *not* terrorism. Nor is this an effort to blackmail anyone. We do have a message that needs to be heard. So we can't turn the *Domino* and all that she symbolizes back over to Admiralty control just yet. We need this 'formidable weapons system,' as you just called it, to help get an even more formidable message out—a message of complete and verifiable nuclear disarmament."

"The news of your action is certainly getting out, Commander," Prim observes. "But aside from evading capture by the Royal Navy and the Marines, who seem intent on doing just that, what are your longer-range hopes and plans?"

"We would like to provoke a dialogue—a debate in Parliament and in the streets of the UK—as soon as possible: a dialogue about British leadership in nuclear disarmament. In the long run, depending on how the political winds blow, we will either surrender the *Domino* to a government-sponsored disarmament process, hopefully monitored by the U.N., or we will seek security and safe harbor for the *Domino* and for ourselves in a neutral country sympathetic to our position on nuclear disarmament and willing to work with us."

"Specifically what message would you like the government and people of the UK to hear at this time? Do you have any specific *requests*?"

"I'm glad you're using that word, Leslie, making the distinction between *requests* and *demands*. In addition to our request that Parliament waste no time debating unilateral nuclear disarmament, there is one further request regarding personnel. It's about how we, the messengers, shall be treated by those in military authority who may not like either our message or our methods."

Turning to his Executive Officer, Richard Hartwell, McGinty asks, "Richard, have you got our *requests* typed up?"

"Yes, Sir," replies Hartwell, who hands a copy of some sheets of paper to Prim. He explains, "Our main request is to have the UK lead the world toward total nuclear disarmament, and to lead by example. . . No human being, and in particular no British soldier, should ever be ordered to launch the weapons we carry. We want the UK to set an example of complete, verifiable, and if necessary unilateral nuclear disarmament that hopefully all other nuclear states will quickly follow."

"Do you expect the United States to follow the UK's lead?" asks Prim.

Hartwell thinks for a moment, then replies, "That's beyond our ability to predict... probably not initially. France, on the other hand, could easily join us in making the E.U. nuclear-weapons-free. And then we could use our collective leverage to secure the disarmament of other nuclear-armed states who might wish to secure more favorable diplomatic and trade relations with the E.U. India and Pakistan could probably be persuaded... even Israel."

McGinty, smiling, raises his finger and adds, "But it would be fun to imagine the nuclear weapons establishment in the US being swept along, too... even swept away, in a worldwide paradigm shift." He grins mischievously. "There are a great many voices in the US calling for this very thing... Just have a look at the Nuclear Age Peace Foundation Web site. We don't think our friends in the US will be ignoring us."

Turning to Hartwell, McGinty invites him to continue.

"Secondly," Hartwell says, "we would like amnesty for our officers and crew. By amnesty, we mean simply having the government recognize that we acted in good conscience, consistent with international law. We acted for the good of humanity. If we are ultimately judged unfit to continue to work for a nuclear-weapons-free Royal Navy, then surely we deserve nothing worse than summary discharge from our military commitments."

After a moment of thoughtful silence on Leslie's part, McGinty comments, "Leslie... you should know that Dick has a law background, so he added a footnote to the second request that I think deserves attention."

Turning to Hartwell, he asks, "Dick, can you read that footnote?"

"Here's what I added," he replies, passing another sheet to Leslie:

> Note: If her majesty's government flatly declines amnesty for us, then we seek guarantees that any prosecution, if pursued, will be appealable to either (a.) the European Court of Human Rights, under Section 1, Article 2, Right to Life, which criminalises any government's use of force that is 'more than absolutely necessary' to defend itself from unlawful violence; or (b.) the International Criminal Court, under Article 8, War Crimes, Section 2 - b - 4, which defines a war crime as: 'Intentionally launching an attack in the knowledge that such attack will cause incidental loss of life or injury to civilians or damage to civilian objects or widespread, long-term and severe damage to the natural environment which would be clearly excessive in relation to the concrete and direct overall military advantage anticipated.'

Prim observes, "So you are *requesting* changes in defence policy requiring the attention of nothing less than the highest levels of the British government... Yet there is no threat on your part to do anything if the government refuses. What happens if the Royal Navy attacks or disables you?"

"Miss Prim," McGinty interjects, "for the record, this is neither an armed confrontation nor a terrorist action. While we have the capability, we are making absolutely no threats to launch missiles at anyone. But since we have an obligation to protect our own lives and the weapons systems aboard the *Domino*, and to avoid at all cost a release of radioactive material, the crew intends to evade and counter any efforts by any state to seize or disable this vessel. Since we pose no threat, we hope there will be no rash military actions ordered that would endanger the integrity of this vessel or the well-being of its crew... Now, please excuse me, I need to set a new course." McGinty rises to exit.

Prim concludes the interview with "Thank you, Commander McGinty, and thank you, Officer Hartwell. Aboard the Vanguard-class Trident submarine, *Vengeance*, renamed the *Domino*, somewhere in the English Channel, this is Leslie Prim for BBC television news."

She motions to Josh to cut the recording.

Wednesday afternoon, 15:00 GMT.

Madam Prime Minister of the UK is in her office at 10 Downing Street, watching the television news and learning more about the incident off the coast at Brighton. The BBC News Anchor is concluding his report:

> . . . after the BBC camera crew skidded onto the deck in a zodiac, they were hustled into a hatch. Soon a Royal Marine helicopter attempted to lower some marines onto the sub to reestablish control, but the *Vengeance* slipped beneath the waves and vanished.

An intercom buzzes; the PM mutes her telly. A secretary's voice announces, "The Secretary of State for Defence and his entourage are here."

"Send them in," replies the PM. Strong and Rakewell enter with about a half-dozen high-ranking staff.

The PM greets them and gestures to the telly, still showing pictures of the submarine. "Well, gentlemen, news of the *affaire*

Vengeance—let's not call it an insurrection yet—is rapidly spreading around the world, as you can see. What *are* we going to do about it?"

She switches off the television, and they all move to a conference table. "Admiral Rakewell," she begins, "can you give us an update?"

"At this time we know that the *Vengeance* is submerged somewhere off our southern coast, Madam, and we are trying to track her. But it's difficult because those subs are nearly silent and the crew are trained to avoid detection. We are using all available means to communicate with them. They must be hearing us, but they are not responding."

"Well … can you disable her in some safe way and force her to the surface?" she inquires.

Marshall Strong, Secretary of State for Defence, himself an ex-Royal Navy admiral, responds. "Of course we could attempt to torpedo her with a crippling rather than a lethal charge, but that would risk the release of highly radioactive fuel and fissionable material. Am I right, gentlemen?"

The officers nod in agreement.

After a moment of reflection Strong adds, "Absent the threat of attack—and there is none, attempting to disable the *Vengeance* by depth charge or torpedo seems unwise. So far, madam, only one military law has been broken, namely the failure of the *Vengeance* to acknowledge and reply to communications. Technically there is no mutiny, since Commander McGinty and his officers and crew all seem to be acting in unison.

The PM asks, "Does the crew of the *Vengeance* even have the ability to arm and launch her missiles without the appropriate launch codes being transmitted by me?"

Rakewell chimes in, "Officially they can't, Madam. But as we know, the Commanders of all our missile subs have the ability to launch their weapons in extraordinary situations, provided that they can secure the cooperation of their two launch officers, each with his own key. But it appears that launching those missiles is precisely what Cmdr. McGinty and his crew intend to avoid doing under any circumstances, so we can probably rest easy on that score."

"Very well," Madam PM remarks. "Then continue to pursue the sub. Track it— just don't attack it."

Wednesday afternoon, 15:30 GMT.

Back aboard the *Domino*, after McGinty's departure for the bridge, Prim has been chatting with Executive Officer Hartwell. Her cameraman, Josh, is checking over the previous video recordings, as he prepares to record another interview.

Speaking softly to Hartwell, Prim inquires, "Richard... off the record... do you know where we're going? This is the first time I've been on a nuclear sub."

"My guess is that the skipper is taking more evasive maneuvers. He's probably also thinking about where and how to put you and your cameraman back safely ashore again. Where would you like to be let off? Back in Brighton? The Orkneys?"

Prim pauses as their eyes meet. There's a hint of a smile that crosses her lips. "Well what's the rush? There may be some advantages to all concerned if I stay around to report this adventure, especially if I can periodically relay my stories to a BBC affiliate. Is there a way I can do that from the sub?"

"When we're on routine deployment and relations with the Russians are normal," Richard replies, "we periodically do let the crew use the internet to transmit e-mail, sound files, and YouTube-quality video. But in recent weeks we have been maintaining radio silence, so as not to disclose our location. We might, however, be able to arrange to send your latest video interviews ashore tonight with a volunteer."

Hartwell turns toward Josh, the cameraman. "Josh, does your camera use standard mini-DV cassettes? Or memory cards?"

"Standard SD cards... but I've got only one spare. Have you got a few extra on board?"

"I'm sure we can borrow some from the crew."

Turning to Prim, Hartwell says, "Sorry, Leslie. Would you like to continue doing interviews?"

"Oh yes!" she replies, "Let's! But I really would like to personalize my reportage, by bringing some new faces in front of the camera; not necessarily officers in the chain of command. Can you suggest anyone else? And could we change the venue?"

"Let me call Chaplain Matthew," Hartwell suggests. "He has been an important player in this process." Richard goes to the intercom. "Chaplain Matthew, please report to Captain Hartwell in the mess."

He then escorts Leslie and Josh to the mess, which doubles as a lounge and meeting room. He remarks, "Here is where the most important decisions in this affair have been made."

They enter and move to a corner where an interview can be set up. Before long, Chaplain Matthew joins them.

"Hi, Denis... welcome," says Hartwell. "You may have heard that we picked up a BBC television reporter and cameraman when we surfaced off Brighton. Meet Leslie Prim."

She shakes Denis's hand and smiles.

"... and her cameraman, Josh."

"Hello, Josh."

"Pleasure!" Josh replies, reaching over to shake Matthew's hand.

Prim asks, "May we use first names? Hi, I'm Leslie."

"And I'm Denis."

She gestures for Denis to sit next to her in front of the camera. Prim holds a microphone as the TV camera starts to record.

"This is Leslie Prim, reporting aboard the Trident missile submarine SSBN *Vengeance*, Wednesday at about 15:45 GMT. The crew of this sub have renamed her the *Domino* for reasons which I think will become clear in this interview. I'm in the all-purpose room called the mess, and to my left is the Chaplain of the vessel, Rev. Denis Matthew. Can you explain to us, Denis, what has come over the officers and crew of this nuclear submarine? Why *this* action? And why now?"

"Well... it's been quite a month... We began our silent patrol in the North Atlantic about five weeks ago. I was holding prayer services at dawn and dusk, ship's time, every day, with two services on Sundays to accommodate crew shifts. I began this tour by preaching on the value of family ties. On the first Sunday, I asked each crew member to drop by my quarters during the week, or show up the next Sunday, with a photograph of his family or significant others. On the second Sunday, at the services, we laid all their photos out on adjacent tables in the mess, and I raised my hands and prayed over them, thanking the Creator for all the beautiful souls, young and old, they represented. Then I gave a reflection on the Beatitudes in Matthew's Gospel, Chapter 5, you know, "Blessed are the poor in spirit... Blessed are those who mourn... Blessed are the peacemakers, for they will be called Children of God."

Prim responds, "Sounds like pretty radical stuff for a nuclear missile sub!"

Matthew gives her a knowing glance, rolling his eyes. "As you might expect, I talked with many members of the crew. I asked whether what we were doing as peace*keepers*, tending our nation's nuclear trigger, would qualify us as peace*makers*—as Children of God. This got them thinking. I also went through the Lord's Prayer, asking whether the part about our being forgiven to the extent that we forgive others who offend us was compatible with what we were being paid to do aboard the *Vengeance*. Of course, this challenged many in the crew, probably because they hadn't really thought about it before. There was some grumbling. I had a few visits after that Sunday service from crew and officers who wanted to remind me of the need to keep our nuclear deterrent viable to prevent some kind of preemptive destruction of the UK."

Prim remarks, "I'm surprised that you could accept an assignment on a nuclear missile submarine, Denis, feeling the way you do about nuclear deterrence."

"I'll admit," he replies, "I did expect it to be a challenge—but at least a well-paying one. And quite frankly, I'm no different from anyone else aboard this sub in that respect: I needed the money. It's not like there are jobs with comparable pay in parishes out there, just begging to be filled by Anglican priests... especially by those of us who are male clergy these days. But to tell the truth, I didn't realize just how incompatible the lifestyle of a nuclear-missile submariner would be with the Gospel until I enlisted. When one dwells in the deep, the *de profundis* prayer, 'From the depths I cry to you, O Lord. Hear my prayer,' has special resonance. So I did what any chaplain would do who finds himself in a problematic situation. I prayed. I held this sub and her entire crew up to God in prayer from the depths. And the rest of the time I simply did my duty as a Royal Navy Chaplain. I was a good listener."

"Yes, but as the ship's Chaplain, when you saw the effect that your preaching was having, did you back off? Or did you pursue it?" Prim asks.

"What I really did was to cool it—to withdraw a bit, into the desert, so to speak. I gathered a number of sailors around me who were already responding to the Gospel call not to retaliate. These fellows were beginning to feel 'troubled in spirit,' as scripture puts it—alienated from their official duties, and even from their own deepest selves. We began to meet as small groups at various times and simply to pray through all this. We asked for the guidance of the Spirit. It seems that the whole issue of retaliation—of nuclear revenge, if you will—became a growing topic of discussion among the crew and officers when they were not on duty practicing the targeting and firing of those damned missiles."

"Still," Prim notes, "it's a long way from discussion to action. How did the officers and crew move from thinking... to... to what some would call an insurrection?"

Other sailors in the mess are gradually drifting over to where the interview is being held, peering over the head of the seated cameraman, and quietly listening.

Denis continues, "The collective change of heart seems to have occurred gradually. But I will say this: we have a group of sailors who are into putting on skits! A few weeks ago they were imitating boys from Kansas aboard a 'boomer,' the slang the Yanks use for their Trident submarines. These yokels were trying to figure out the orders they thought they received to launch their missiles against St. Petersburg. When they looked up the name in their computers, the only St. Petersburg they could find was in Florida."

Laughter and guffaws erupt from the on looking sailors.

"And so," Denis continues, "the notion of thinking twice about launch orders, and questioning the wisdom and morality of nuclear retaliation, were really coming out of the closet. All three crew shifts got to see the Boomer skit, by the way, and it just fanned the flames of doubt about what in God's name—or more precisely our country's name—we were being paid for and expected to do."

Wednesday afternoon, 16:00 GMT.

McGinty enters the mess. Someone shouts, "Officer on deck!" and all stand. He says "At ease!" The interviewees gesture to him to come and join them. Carrying a clipboard, McGinty takes a seat to the right of Prim. The video-interview resumes.

Leslie continues, "Hello again, Commander McGinty, and welcome to this second interview aboard the SSBN *Vengeance*, now called the *Domino*. We have just been hearing from Chaplain Matthew about how your officers and crew went through some serious soul-searching over the last few weeks. May I put this next question to you both? At what point did the doubt turn into a decision to act? And was it truly unanimous?"

McGinty reflects for a moment, and then offers this recollection. "About a week ago, after hearing Chaplain Matthew's reflections, and after discussing the issues with many of my officers and crew, it became clear to me that it was highly unlikely that I could rely on any of them—and I'm talking in particular about my missile officers and crew, the ones who target and launch the Tridents—to actually launch any of our missiles, even if the PM herself issued a direct order. It was like the wind had shifted aboard the submarine. And, I must say, there was a contagious sense of relief for many that the change we were experiencing was finally getting out into the open. It affected me, too. I'm no 'turn the other cheek' guy, but when the stakes get this high, and you know as much about these weapons as I do, nuclear retaliation looks increasingly like insanity! So I decided to test what I perceived to be happening. I drew up a resolution to put to a vote of the officers and crew after last Sunday's services."

McGinty consults his clipboard, and reads from it.

> Resolved: The Officers and Crew of SSBN *Vengeance*, recognizing that nuclear warfare is genocidal and therefore illegal under all existing international laws and treaties, hereby declare that we will not participate in the launching of any of the nuclear missiles we currently carry against any place or places on planet Earth, under any circumstances.

The Skipper continues, "I called for a vote by saying, 'All in favor signify by saying Aye!' The 'ayes' were loud, strong... even overwhelming. When I asked for 'nays,' I didn't hear a thing. As far as I was concerned, that vote was the beginning of the end of the SSBN *Vengeance* as a tool for nuclear revenge. There would be no more pretending from then on. We had to be honest with ourselves. It's important for me as a skipper to know what I can and can't expect of my officers and crew. And it's only honest that my superiors be made aware of the situation."

Turning to Matthew, Leslie asks, "May I inquire, then, how you moved from deciding what you would *not* do, to deciding what you *would* do?"

He replies, "After that vote, the skipper offered the crew a few reflections of his own on where we could go from here. He said it didn't make sense to continue our tour of duty at sea in silence for two more months, acting like nothing had changed, and then just

26

quietly return the *Vengeance* to her base in Scotland, only to have her re-provisioned and sent out again with the Starboard Crew. We're the Port Crew, by the way, and we take turns manning the sub every three months."

"The skipper suggested that we might consider using our sub, which is uniquely self-sufficient, as an attention-getter, to force a wider discussion of real nuclear disarmament, first in the UK, and eventually worldwide. He acknowledged that this action could cost us all our jobs, and that the outcome would determine whether we would be greeted as heroes or condemned as insurrectionists. But he also said, and I think he's right, that if we continue to think more of the good of everyone on earth, rather than our own paychecks, we might just come out of this sharing the Nobel Peace Prize."

Denis adds, "Forgive me if I digress here for a moment, but as a clergy-person, I associate what was happening to this crew with the centuries-old tradition of baptism." He gestures down and up with his hands. "It's like we went down into the water and died to our old selves, and now are coming up to new life. Others, of course, see this as our best humanitarian instincts coming out after an experience of enlightenment. It really doesn't matter how we interpret it—the fact is, we have nearly all had a profound change of heart... From my perspective as a person of faith, I reckon it to be a miracle."

Prim checks her perception by restating what she heard. "So your skipper proposed that the officers and crew think about using the *Vengeance* as a kind of bully pulpit, to make strong public statements."

"Yes. And at that point," Denis continues, "I cautioned them that this was going to be a very serious next step. 'Proclaiming the good news,' and 'freeing slaves,' to use the language of the Bible, is never without controversy. Assuming the prophet's mantle could cost us a great deal. So I proposed that we—that each crew shift—should meet again in 24 hours to vote on the matter of going public. Meanwhile, the skipper promised that he would draft and post in the mess hall a resolution about future actions, in such a way that everyone could read it, offer revisions, think about it, and decide whether to support it or not. He also pinned an envelope on the board where anyone who wanted to opt out of this next phase of protest could quietly drop his name, and the skipper would find a way to set them ashore."

"I thought this was a particularly considerate thing to do," Denis adds, "because in any group of 120-odd men you are going to find some with less inclination than others to claim the moral high ground. I mean, if you're in this job for the money and house payments are due, you don't jeopardize your employment lightly. I fully expected ten or twenty percent to defect at this point. But my small prayer groups kept praying. Skipper, why don't you take the story from here?"

McGinty clears his throat. "Here's a copy of the draft resolution I posted." He reads it aloud.

RESOLUTION

We the Officers and Crew of the SSBN *Vengeance*, being of sound mind and body, and having decided for the love of our brothers and sisters in the human family not to launch our nuclear weapons against any nation or people under any circumstances, do hereby commit ourselves:

a. to make public our dissent by periodic surfacing and media contact, aimed at drawing attention to the insanity of nuclear weapons,

b. to use every means available to call for prompt government debate and action on British unilateral nuclear disarmament,

c. to defend this vessel from any effort by any state or group to seize it or exploit its nuclear weapons; and

d. to peacefully deliver this vessel, renamed the *Domino*, to a government that will offer us asylum and be committed to the deactivation and destruction of its nuclear weapons in the interest of world peace.

"How did the next 24 hours go?" Leslie asks. "Was the statement received as well as you expected?"

McGinty replies, "There were some suggestions to simply scuttle the sub and all her missiles, and apply for asylum with a neutral country. But in the end the crew and officers decided to go with the resolution I just read."

"Were there any dissenters who put their names in that 'opt out' envelope?"

"There were nine—none of whom had actual missile-launching responsibility anyway. They were guys who just wanted to do their jobs and not make waves. We set them ashore last night off the village of Salcombe, near Plymouth. We wish them well... and that brings us to today!"

"Yes," replies Prim, "and where do you all go from here?"

She hears McGinty state very calmly, "We have another two months' provisions and all the water and air we need to maintain ourselves. And we have work to do! We'll be monitoring the media on various frequencies, including short wave, to see how our peace action is being received."

"And how will you avoid being captured or disabled?" asks Prim.

McGinty replies, "We are still not responding to the usual military communication frequencies, and we plan to remain silent and hidden between our manifestations on the surface... how did you suggest calling these surfacings, Denis?"

"Oh ... our *epiphanies*," replies the chaplain. There is laughter among the nearby crew.

Leslie concludes her interview with, "Thank you, Commander McGinty, and Chaplain Matthew. For BBC Television News, this is Leslie Prim, reporting from the SSBN *Domino* deep beneath the Channel."

She continues staring into the camera with her customary, ironic half-smile until Josh stops recording. Then she turns to McGinty.

"Off the record, Commander, can I ask you where we're going? and how I can deliver this flash-card or its contents to the BBC?"

"Initially we dove and continued on an easterly course toward Dover, but more recently I've made a wide turn and we're now heading at high speed toward the Irish sea. In a couple of hours we'll be off the Isle of Man, which has a BBC station. What I'll probably do is approach Castletown or Douglas at dusk, depending on the ferry traffic, and set you and your cameraman ashore in an inflatable. Will that work for you?"

Prim takes a minute to consult with Josh, her cameraman, then turns to McGinty. "If I can arrange to stay with you for a few more days, Commander, I'd like to stick around to see this story through, as a reporter. Josh, my cameraman, says he'll be happy to bring his flash-drive ashore this evening. He'll arrange to drop it off with a BBC-TV affiliate. He could also probably rendezvous with us again some evening if we tell him where and when, to pick up more of our recordings. Does that sound fair?"

"That's a good plan!" says McGinty. "We've never had a woman among the crew, Leslie. We'll deal with it as best we can. I've got the only private room, so I'll give you my quarters."

McGinty then turns toward Hartwell. "Richard, let's give Josh some GPS coordinates off Falmouth, and plan to meet him there in three days, say Sunday at 23:00 hours, to deliver more recordings. Be sure he has your mobile phone number and we have his, because we may need it to contact him in the interim. Have him bring to the next rendezvous some hard copies of any press reports covering government and popular reactions to our little adventure."

As the group disperses, Richard begins to show Leslie around the submarine, chatting amicably with her and introducing her to various crew members as they move about. He points out the operations center, the bridge, the communications suite, and the sonar and countermeasures area. Then he leads her to her new quarters in the skipper's cabin, where they sit and talk quietly for a time—a surprisingly long time.

CHAPTER 3

PURSUIT AND EVASION

Flotillas are pretty but useless,
Such little boats reckoned as fruitless,
But at Dunkirk we know
How they managed to show
That small tigers are not always toothless.

Wednesday afternoon, 17:00 GMT.

Back at Northwood, once again in the Situation Room, Admiral Rakewell has just convened a meeting of the Navy Board, which includes Nigel Hodgson, Commander-in-Chief Fleet (CINCFLEET), Rodney Bremner, Chief of Strategic Systems Executive (CSSE), and a half-dozen other senior officers. There is a large electronic map of the British Isles and surrounding waters on the wall, with indications of where various Royal Navy submarines and surface ships are located.

Rakewell speaks first. "Thank you, Gentlemen, for coming on such short notice. We have a crisis on our hands, and it has gone public. Let's have an update on the mutiny of the SSBN *Vengeance*." He nods to Hodgson. "Admiral?"

Hodgson replies, "Sir, our helicopter was unable to land Marines on the *Vengeance* this afternoon, off Brighton, because she dove. The helicopter crew tried to trace her movement underwater with listening buoys, but noise from the small craft in the area made that impossible. Those boats were reported as actively trying to interfere with our pursuit. The *Vengeance* seems to have moved rapidly east, deploying counter-measures that led to our loss of contact. We have no idea where she is now, but we have alerted our anti-submarine forces to try to locate and track her. My guess is that she may be headed for a neutral country with deep water to hide in, like Norway."

With a grimace, Admiral Rakewell turns to his Executive Officer. "Contact the Norwegian Naval Command, and see what kind of cooperation you can secure from them if SSBN *Vengeance* does show up there. Our first priority is to regain control of that sub, regardless of what her insubordinate, delusional crew think they are doing."

"Hodgson," Rakewell asks, "can you give me an idea of how much longer the *Vengeance* can continue without coming in for provisions?"

"Sir, her current provisioning will carry her for two more months... comfortably. By letting off crew, which she evidently has just started doing, she could double or triple that time."

"Is there any way we can disable her without risking either loss of the sub or radiation release?" asks Hodgson, nodding to Rodney Bremner for a response.

Putting a schematic of a Vanguard class SSBN on the screen, Bremner replies. "Sir, we believe it would be possible to disable the *Vengeance* without a high risk of radiation release in two ways— first (pointing to the propeller) by hitting her propeller or rudders. Having one of our attack submarines fire a dummy Spearfish torpedo, defused, at the *Vengeance* from behind, might cause a mechanical collision astern that would put the *Vengeance*'s propeller and steering out of commission. The second method might be by puncturing her skin with something like 50-caliber rounds. She would need to be strafed while on the surface, so the RAF may need to be involved. A punctured hull would probably preclude her diving. Either method could cause casualties and, at worse, radiation leakage, flooding, and loss of the sub."

"Thank you for your suggestions, Rod," says Rakewell. "For the time being let's avoid attacking, while we wait for further sightings and perhaps a chance to negotiate. Are all available communication channels open? What kind of messages are we sending her?"

Bremner replies, "Sir, SSBN *Vengeance* has maintained silence throughout this crisis. The only signal coming from her today was a mobile phone conversation between Cmdr. McGinty and the BBC reporter in Brighton. We assume that the *Vengeance*, even though she's not responsive, is receiving our coded transmissions ordering her to return to her home base. We have already threatened all her officers with hell to pay for insubordination, and demanded that they acknowledge our orders. But to no avail."

Rakewell then asks, "What about that BBC Reporter who went aboard? How will she be relaying her stories? Can we intercept them in the name of national security, to prevent any more inflammatory reports getting out?"

He looks around... silence prevails.

"Will the *Vengeance* crew try to return her—the reporter— to Brighton? Or will they relay her reports by some sort of radio frequency?" Again there is silence.

Under his breath, Rakewell chides the group. "Oh, come on, people! Probably they'll just opt to use one of their damned mobile phones again." A few heads nod, but no one responds.

Turning to Hodgson the Admiral asks, "Hodgson, can your staff get us a list of all mobile phones registered to crew members and likely to be aboard the *Vengeance*? We ought to be able to get a fix on any of them as soon as it is turned on." Hodgson gives an affirmative nod.

Standing, Rakewell addresses the entire group, raising the pitch of his voice as he states, "I don't need to remind you all that this incident is an extreme embarrassment to the Royal Navy and to the Nation. As you are well aware, the new Prime Minister has not yet blocked what the Blair government, of happy memory, allocated years ago for the next generation of nuclear missile submarines."

As he paces to and fro, Rakewell pauses to remind the group of some bigger issues. "We don't want incidents like this to raise questions about our priorities and budgets, let alone the reliability of our Vanguard fleet!" After a moment he adds, "Stay reachable, because we will be meeting again on short notice... Very well! Dismissed."

Wednesday evening, 22:00 GMT

McGinty, Hartwell, and Prim are gathered on the bridge with Josh, who is putting on a life jacket, while crewmembers in the tower are preparing to deploy an inflatable raft to enable him to slip to shore undetected. The helmsman says "Sir, we're a thousand meters off the Isle of Man, just south of Castletown.

McGinty calls out, "Sonar report?"

"No approaching vessels, Sir."

McGinty raises the periscope and does a 360-degree sweep.

"All clear," he states. "Up three more meters, do a radar sweep and report."

After a moment, the radar man reports, "Radar only detecting commercial aviation and coastal ferry traffic, sir."

McGinty orders the helmsman to bring the sub's deck to just above water level, ahead dead slow, and signals to Hartwell to deploy the raft.

The sailors help Josh to climb aboard, and then launch the inflatable. He rows quietly toward shore, his SD-card tucked away in an inside shirt pocket. Hartwell and the sailors duck back inside the submarine and secure the hatch.

Wednesday evening, 22:20 GMT.

As the *Domino* slips beneath the waves, McGinty gives his helmsman new orders. "Lay a course of 210 degrees and follow the ocean floor down to a depth of 120 meters, at one-quarter speed. Then follow the waypoints I punch in. We're heading quietly for the Outer Hebrides. We're going to hide among the rocks near Leverburgh, and there we'll catch the morning news."

After McGinty punches in the waypoint coordinates, he tells the duty officer on the bridge that he'll be bunking with Chaplain Matthew. "Call me there if I'm needed."

Thursday morning, 0800 GMT

The *Domino* has reached the rock formations off Leverburgh, and is lurking in one of the troughs. An antenna has been floated to the surface to permit radio reception. As the crew begin to eat breakfast, the familiar sound of news from a local BBC station is patched through the intercom:

> Our top story continues to be the rogue nuclear missile submarine, the SSBN *Vengeance*. We learned yesterday from BBC reporter Leslie Prim, live on the Brighton waterfront, that the crew have renamed the submarine the *Domino*. Let's replay that segment from her exclusive interview with Commander McGinty:
>
> "What kind of demands are you making, if any, Commander?"
>
> "No demands. Only a request. By going public with our dissent, we hope to start a genuine reversal of the nuclear arms race. We want Britain to lead a worldwide disarmament process, and we've decided to kick-start the process. I guess you could say we're trying to be the first nuclear domino to fall... and we hope that, with our

nudge, all the rest will topple, too."

The crew applaud; some shout "Yeah!" "Right on!"

> "Commander... are you saying that the entire crew and officers are with you on this?"
>
> "Affirmative. It might be more accurate to say that I'm with them. We set nine dissenters ashore earlier today, with no hard feelings; the rest of our crew— about 120 sailors—are hanging together on this."

There is more applause and foot-stomping from the crew. Prim enters the mess. She waves and smiles amid the applause. The BBC report continues with Prim's voice:

> "We've got a close-up of your submarine now, Commander. Is that name hanging on the conning tower, *Domino*, a reference to what you said about dominos toppling? Or is there another, perhaps theological, overtone?"
>
> "You can take it either way. We think that the *Domino*, as a name, says more clearly what we're up to than the *Vengeance*. ... Don't you agree?"
>
> "It does sound a lot less menacing. Have you already rechristened your sub with its new name, Commander?"
>
> "Affirmative. All we're missing is the Champagne... and that may yet come!"

More cheers and applause erupt from the crew. But they quickly hush as the BBC news anchor's voice continues:

> Last night the submarine, which took an evasive dive off Brighton shortly after reporter Leslie Prim was taken aboard, resurfaced somewhere off the Isle of Man and one or more of the crew apparently slipped ashore with fresh TV footage taken aboard the vessel. Those taped interviews with the Commander of the sub,

Executive Officer Hartwell, and the Chaplain, Matthew, will be broadcast in their entirety after our regular nine AM newscast. The skipper of the *Vengeance*—or the *Domino*, as she is now called—Commander McGinty, did reassure the world about the peaceful intentions of his officers and crew. Here's more of Leslie Prim's interview, recorded somewhere in the English channel yesterday afternoon, after the sub took evasive measures.

"Commander, tell us in your own words what is happening. Is it accurate to call this action a hijacking?"

"We want the British authorities and the world to know that we are certainly not hijacking anything. This is *not* terrorism. Nor is this an effort to blackmail anyone. We do have a message that needs to be heard. So we can't turn the *Domino* and all that she symbolizes back over to Admiralty control just yet. We need this 'formidable weapons system,' as you just called it, to help get an even more formidable message out—a message of world peace."

The crew again erupts in applause and cheers, quieting down as Leslie's voice continues:

"The news of your action is certainly getting out, Commander. But aside from evading capture by the Royal Navy and the Marines, who seem intent on doing just that, what are your longer-range hopes and plans?"

"We would like to provoke a dialogue—a debate in Parliament and in the streets of the UK—as soon as possible: a dialogue about British leadership in nuclear disarmament. In the long run, depending on how the political winds blow, we will either surrender the *Domino* to a UK-sponsored disarmament process, or we will seek security and safe harbor for the *Domino* and for ourselves in a neutral country sympathetic to our position on nuclear disarmament, and willing to work with us."

The BBC news anchor continues:

> Reaction from around the world has run the gamut from apprehension to wild enthusiasm. Demonstrations for nuclear disarmament, in solidarity with the *Domino*'s crew, have been announced today in Trafalgar Square and in Hyde Park. Similar gatherings have been called for in most other large cities of the UK.

There is more applause and cheering from the crew, as the news anchor continues:

> The Internet is crackling with e-mailed proposals for demonstrations worldwide to support the men of the *Domino*, praising their action, and calling on the British government to treat this event as a real turning point—a chance to begin to put the nuclear weapons genie back in the bottle.

There is a roar of approval from the crew.

> Church authorities have even weighed in. The Archbishop of Canterbury, the US Conference of Catholic Bishops, and the Vatican have all released statements supporting the call for British—and eventually world—nuclear disarmament . . .
> In other news . . .

The volume fades. Flashing lights suddenly alert crew to maintain silence and head for battle stations. On the bridge, Hartwell, the Executive Officer, and technicians are listening to sonar coming from an attack submarine as it approaches their location.

"Can you tell whose sub it is?" asks Hartwell to his sonar man.

He replies in a half-whisper, "Not yet, sir. Probably one of ours. It seems to have the signature of a Swiftsure or Trafalgar Class SSN, and it is definitely sweeping the area to its front. We're pretty well invisible surrounded by these rocks, so if we remain silent we may be undetected."

The crew remain very still. As they listen, sonar pings begin to lower in pitch, and then to fade. As the threat passes them by, Hartwell quietly asks McGinty, "Sir, you don't think they would actually attack us, do you?"

"Probably not, at least not without a positive ID. But they would love to put an attack sub on our tail just to keep track of us. And it's possible that they would try to put us out of commission by some mechanical means, like fouling our propeller or disabling our rudders. They might even try to puncture our skin with bullets if they catch us on the surface, in the open. So when we come up again, we're going to have to do it within a circle of civilian boats for protection as well as publicity."

Prim enters the bridge area, and McGinty turns to her. "Oh Leslie—nice bit of reportage! Thanks for getting the message out."

"Couldn't have done it without you, Commander!" she replies. "Have you decided on your next destination?"

"Since we have two and a half days to kill before we rendezvous with your cameraman, Josh, off Falmouth, I'm planning to take her around Ireland and southeast past Finistère, to a French island, either Belle-Ile or the Ile d'Yeu, where we expect that we'll be well received and can stage another *epiphany*, as Denis calls our surface happenings. But first I'd like to send a volunteer ashore with a few of our crew's mobile phones, to place strategic phone calls every night from a different coastal location along the west coast of Ireland. Why can't the mice confuse the cat, after all?"

Turning to Hartwell, he asks, "Dick, can you poll the crew to see how many viable mobiles we have aboard, and see if you can get three or four owners to lend them to us for use as decoys? I'll see if I can get our good Chaplain to volunteer for shore duty, to relay greetings to the respective families from strategic locations around the Irish coast... and we'll let our friends at Defence Intelligence, DIS, try to make sense of the unexpected coastal mobile-phone clues that come their way.

"I'm on it, Sir," Hartwell replies as he exits.

Turning back to Prim, McGinty asks, "Leslie, why don't we head back to the mess to listen to the complete broadcast coming at 09:00?"

"Avec plaisir!"

She smiles at him and precedes him off the bridge.

CHAPTER 4

THE WIDENING CIRCLE,
OR
NINEVEH LISTENING

When the populace heard of the stance
Of the sailors who took off their pants,
There were cheers in the streets,
There were twitters and tweets,
And street theatre, music, and dance!

Demonstrators are gathering in the vicinity of 10 Downing Street, the Prime Minister's residence. Some are beating on noisemakers, some carrying placards in favor of nuclear disarmament; all are supporting the *Domino*. A rhythmic chant starts up:

"*Domino, Domino*, no more nukes!"

"*Domino, Domino*, no more nukes!"

"*Domino, Domino*, no more nukes!"

At that very moment, an emergency cabinet meeting is getting under way at the request of Madam Prime Minister (PM). She has summoned the top naval brass, specifically Strong, Secretary of State for Defence; Rakewell, First Sea Lord; and Admiral Hodgson,

CINCFLEET, for a briefing. They are seated at one end of a large table at which ten cabinet Ministers have taken their places.

Standing at the head of the table, the PM opens the meeting: "Thank you all for coming on such short notice. I presume that most of you saw or heard the interviews in the last hour with the officers of SSBN *Vengeance,* aired on BBC-TV. You know of their well-publicized and apparently conscientious action to urge this government to undertake unilateral nuclear disarmament."

After the nods and murmurs around the room subside, she adds, "I am sure that there are a variety of responses to these developments in the minds of the Ministers here present. This action has provoked a huge outpouring of support among the anti-nuclear groups. There were candlelight vigils in Trafalgar Square and in many cities throughout the UK last night. The *Affaire Domino* has quickly become headline news around the globe."

There are murmurs of agreement. She continues. "The event is producing major political and moral fallout around the world, even as we speak. An international 'Day of Solidarity' with the crew of the sub has been called, this Saturday—it's all over the Internet. Saturday is already being called 'D-Day—*Domino* Day.' Practically every Church leader in Christendom has been speaking out in support of this action. Muslim and Buddhist and Hindu clerics won't be far behind."

Absorbed in her thoughts, she slowly starts to pace around the room. "We even received a few minutes ago a wire from the Vatican. The Pope begged us to seize the moment and lead the world into a new era of peace through nuclear disarmament. As you know, one of my predecessors of unhappy memory pushed through Parliament a controversial funding measure for the complete overhaul and renovation of the UK Trident submarine fleet over about twenty years. There are a lot of jobs hanging on that funding."

After more murmurs of assent are heard, she reminds them, "Our party came to power partly as a reaction against the ever costlier nuclear arms race, but we have not been able to muster the political capital to cancel or redirect the funding already approved for the modernization of the Trident submarine fleet. Consequently, the action of the SSBN *Vengeance* crew has suddenly become a huge political issue, not simply a military embarrassment. I'm going to start by asking Admiral Rakewell to give us the Royal Navy's assessment." She takes her seat, gesturing to him to take the floor.

"Madam Prime Minister, Ladies and Gentlemen, the skipper and crew of the *Vengeance* may have the noblest of intentions, but they are in flagrant violation of military discipline, and for the present have seriously undermined the nuclear deterrent capability of Britain. By refusing to follow orders and by not responding to messages from Fleet Headquarters, they are in direct violation of our code of military conduct and could, in fact, be regarded as insurrectionists. We have summoned every available attack submarine in our fleet back to British territorial waters, because we believe that the *Vengeance* intends to continue surfacing periodically to tout its controversial message of unilateral disarmament. We think we can disable her or prevent her diving, without compromising her nuclear weapons or power plant shielding. But first we need to locate her. The US Navy has been in touch already and has volunteered to reassign some of its own hunter-killer subs to the effort to locate and disable the *Vengeance*. Secretary Strong has been advised of the US offer of help, and is considering it."

Nodding to Strong, the PM invites him to respond. "Marshall, would you please give us your perspective on this?"

"Admiral Rakewell," Strong replies, "is correct that this represents an acute embarrassment to the Royal Navy. It is a serious breach of military discipline, and risks spinning out of control, especially if we get the Yanks involved. So I have not yet invited them in. Given that the actual military threat to the UK and our allies is nil at this moment, I am inclined not to resort to any kind of disabling attack against the *Vengeance*. There is still a reasonable hope that we will get her back intact if we don't force the crew to do something rash. We can certainly require them to keep their heads down, however, while we wait them out. I need not remind anyone of how much these submarines cost, nor of the dangers of a radiation leak."

Hodgson raises his hand. The PM recognizes him.

"Madam Prime Minister, it might be advantageous to lead the officers of the *Vengeance* to think that they are under threat of seizure or disabling attack. It would keep them squarely on the defensive and running, as they are now. If we keep the pressure on, they won't feel they have the freedom to surface and talk with the media as openly as they did before."

"Very well, then," she replies. "It appears that a consensus has formed that our armed forces alone should be dealing with the *Vengeance* affair, so let's keep the Yanks out of this, and far away."

Turning to Hodgson and Rakewell, she affirms, "You'll want to continue sending messages ordering the *Vengeance* back to base, with reminders of the personal and career cost to all who disobey direct orders. Are we in agreement that for the time being no weapons shall be used against her?"

All nod.

"Very well, then. Let's let these Officers return to their duties."

Hodgson and Rakewell depart, as the PM moves over to a window to observe the demonstration outside. The chanting has only gotten stronger, and can be heard in the cabinet room even with the heavy bullet-proof windows shut.

"*Domino, Domino*, no more nukes!"

"*Domino, Domino*, no more nukes!"

"*Domino, Domino*, no more nukes!"

With these faint sounds still audible in the background, the Prime Minister now addresses her cabinet. "Beyond the military dimensions of the problem, we have a large and growing political issue to face. Shall we risk appearing to cave in to blackmail by immediately introducing a bill into Parliament calling for unilateral nuclear disarmament, as the officers and sailors of the *Vengeance* are requesting? Or shall we do the traditional thing and refuse to budge in the face of what some would call blackmail?"

With no one offering an answer, the PM continues. "Since there are no demands as such and no threats, we technically could respond to their primary *request* as if the idea had already been under active discussion. For now the word blackmail, and especially the word terrorism, should not even be mentioned by this government in commenting on this incident. Am I right?"

"Here, here!" echoes around the room, and all nod.

"Very well, then. The choice is ours: to ride this fortuitous wave—to go with the flow, or to stand firmly against it on principle. I'd like to go around the room for your initial assessments. I ask for your most succinct thoughts in one or two sentences please, starting with you, Rodney."

"You are correct that it's not a hijacking, and it's not blackmail we're facing. What's more, they're politely 'requesting' that we do what I believe we all would really like to do anyway, in our heart of hearts—getting rid of those awful weapons."

The second minister, to Rodney's left, observes in turn, "The public are very definitely with the officers and crew of the *Domino*, as they've rechristened the sub." He chuckles at the idea of the name. "If we cooperated, this could be a tremendous political lift for our party... and, dare I say, a watershed moment for the nation and the world."

The third minister, Chancellor of the Exchequer, is quick to point out the obvious. "From the budgetary point of view, Madam, the cessation of funding for all nuclear weapons, including their security and delivery systems, would be an enormous boon to the Exchequer and to the taxpayers of Britain. Need I say more?"

The fourth minister, charged with E.U. relations, adds, "From the perspective of our allies on the Continent, our unilateral nuclear disarmament would be a shock indeed. But maybe it's a shock whose time has come. The cold war is over. Were we to start the nuclear disarmament ball seriously rolling, I can't imagine that the rest of the nuclear-armed states, France in particular, would not follow suit."

The Interior Minister, the fifth respondent, states soberly, "Our party will be eating crow if we start eliminating contracts in the defence sector tied to the new Trident's funding cycles. We had better start thinking of alternative uses for those subs. I wonder if they would be any good for oceanographic research. Or tourism?"

The sixth minister, the Foreign Secretary, enthusiastically states, "The consequences for the UK of unilateral nuclear disarmament, in terms of international good will, could be huge. The Foreign Office has already been getting reports of British consulates being approached by people bearing flowers in response to the *Domino* affair. Imagine that! Flowers instead of car bombs!"

"Speaking off the record," the seventh minister, in charge of intelligence, observes, "MI5 and DIS have been caught entirely off guard by this action. Yesterday morning no one would have anticipated a challenge like this coming from the very heart of the Royal Navy. There are no foreign or subversive elements to blame, unless you consider the Bible to be subversive. Perhaps we should."

Tom, the eighth minister, serves as Britain's Ambassador to the U.N. "It's still too early, New-York time," he notes, "for reaction from the UN. But our staff have gotten wind that resolutions of support for the officers and crew of the *Vengeance*, or the *Domino*, are going to be echoing in the halls of the UN, the General Assembly in particular, later today. At the very least, loud calls for the nuclear-weapon states to recommit themselves to the Non-Proliferation Treaty can be anticipated within the UN. Noisy street demonstrations will probably add to the momentum. Perhaps *we* should be the ones *leading* the charge, rather than just reacting to events."

The ninth minister, Sean, manages intra-governmental relations. "In case anyone is interested, our Parliamentary Liaison staff is already at work drafting various wordings of a Bill that would commit this government to systematic, verifiable, and rapid nuclear disarmament. I think there's a lot of wonderful PR that could come of this... if it were pitched just right."

The PM stands again, and starts pacing, rubbing her chin thoughtfully. "Don't get up. I just want to think on my feet for a moment... I can see that there is already considerable sentiment in favor of nuclear arms elimination—not just rollback. Where do you think we might encounter the greatest opposition if we were to move seriously in that direction? Rodney?"

He replies, "It's hard to predict, but the staunchest Tories in both houses of Parliament, especially those with constituencies whose jobs would be threatened, can be expected to howl in opposition... purely for the loss of jobs and contracts, of course."

Raising his hand, and being recognized by the PM, Strong strikes a cautionary note. "We have a military-industrial complex whose members and friends, including influential ones in North America, will not mince words in condemning a government that kowtows to blackmail. They could spin this episode rather ruthlessly against us, and lambaste our *naïveté*, if they wished."

"I know," says the PM. "We have to counter that threat convincingly if we are going to sail with the wind on this one!" She then gestures to Rebecca. "Any commercial implications?"

Rebecca Courtney, whose portfolio includes foreign trade, responds, "My department's best guess is that British prestige, and the rise in stature of all things British abroad, including—forgive my sounding facetious—the new-found British values of non-violence and solidarity with the human family: all this could easily translate into preferential treatment for British goods by our trading partners."

Raising his hand, Tom, the UN Ambassador, adds, "Not only that, but there's already a group of 150 or so stable, economically developed states, all without nuclear weapons—they're sometimes referred to as the Middle Powers. They have been consistently voting in the General Assembly against nuclear weapons for years. If we wished, we could try to organize those states, indeed *all* the anti-nuclear-weapon states, into a kind of new Commonwealth—a new trading bloc. In fact, the name NDC, or the Nuclear Disarmament

Coalition, has already been suggested for such a bloc. Imagine the economic and moral leverage that such a coalition could muster against any state that resisted the call to complete and verifiable nuclear and WMD disarmament!"

The PM, after a thoughtful pause, acknowledges the drift of the dialogue. "I'm getting a consensus here that this government should seriously consider endorsing the concept of unilateral nuclear disarmament... We might even let it be known that we've had it in our hopper for months, and are welcoming the opportunity finally to go public with it."

She strokes her chin, pensively, while pacing. "But we'll have to bring Parliament along with us. And of course I'll have to brief the Queen."

Turning to Sean, she asks, "Sean, could you please have those draft bills you mentioned on my desk by noon? And see that the other cabinet members receive review copies."

"Yes, Ma'am, that should be possible by noon or one o'clock at the latest."

"Right... and as I think about it," says the PM, looking at Strong, "let's go easy on the officers and crew of the *Vengeance*. We may want to relay to them that they are no longer in danger of imminent attack... although I do hope we can locate and track them."

The PM walks back to the head of the table, and continues, "Instead of threatening courts martial, have Hodgson tell them that they are still under orders to return to their base at Faslane, but that their disarmament request is being seriously considered by the PM and the Cabinet."

To the other Cabinet members, she says, "I don't think they will surrender the sub yet, but at least they will know that their request has been heard and that we're thinking about it."

CHAPTER 5

CAT AND MICE CAPERS

Her majesty's finest may groan
At the thought of disarming alone.
They continue to seek
Little mice, who aren't meek,
As they monitor every cell phone.

Thursday evening, 22:00 GMT

Having reached the West coast of Ireland, the *Domino* is slowly entering Donegal Bay, near Bundoran. The weather is overcast, with visibility almost nil in the pitch blackness, save for occasional patches of moonlight. The vessel rises so that its deck is barely above water level. McGinty is briefing Matthew, as some crew members prepare an inflatable to set the chaplain ashore.

"Denis, please remember to get word to the French anti-nuclear groups that a flotilla has to be organized and sent out to meet and escort us for an hour or so. We'll be surfacing just east of Belle-Ile Saturday at 12:00 noon local time, or 11:00 GMT."

McGinty hands Matthew a slip of paper. "Here are the GPS

coordinates; have them form a ring around it and we'll pop up in the center. If they can quietly invite *la presse* but not *la marine*, so much the better."

Matthew replies, "Yes, I'll bet I can do that from any Internet café. I'll fire up the first of the crew mobile phones around an hour after you've left. Then it's off to Galway Friday night for the next call, and down on the Southern Coast of Ireland on Saturday night for the next."

"That should confuse the cats!" says McGinty. "They'll be sniffing for us all along the Atlantic coast. Have you got any plans for after that, say Sunday?"

"I'll try to lie low until it's safe to stick my head up. I'm thinking of fading into the Iona Community for a while. I have friends there who will give me shelter—sanctuary as we churchmen call it. Shall I try to prepare them to give the *Domino* and her crew sanctuary, too?"

"Sanctuary! Now there's a timely concept!"

"Well it worked in the 12th century," opines Matthew, "at least on occasion. Why not try it again?"

"It will have to depend on which way the political winds are blowing. Iona, being in Scotland, is under the Crown. It could be risky. To give us some options, why don't you see if you can find a 'sanctuary' for us on the coast of Ireland? Ireland has always been a staunch foe of nuclear weapons. They could well give us shelter, if it comes to that. So could Canada."

"Yes. Well, I'm off. I'll watch for you in France. *Bon voyage, messieurs!*"

"That's right," says McGinty. "France is next for us. *Bon voyage* to you, too, Denis!"

McGinty waves to him as he rows toward shore. Then Skipper and crew scurry back inside as the *Domino* begins to drop from sight.

Thursday evening, 23:00 GMT

Silently, about an hour later, the sub slips out of Donegal Bay. McGinty, on the bridge, issues orders to the helmsman, while gesturing to a navigation display. "Take her to about 50 kilometers off Penzance and float an antenna. Adjust your arrival time for about 10:45 Friday morning. In the meantime, I'll be catching some sleep in the former Chaplain's quarters."

Turning to the Watch Officer, McGinty says, "Call me if anything detects or pursues us."

"Aye, aye, Sir."

McGinty exits.

Thursday evening, 23:10 GMT

In the Situation Room at Permanent Joint Headquarters, Northwood, a flashing light appears on the screen, this time on the west coast of Ireland. We hear a voice over the intercom. "Code three alert, code three alert: The SSBN *Vengeance* may be off the coast of Bundoran, Ireland. A mobile phone registered to one of the crew has just been activated near Bundoran."

The Northwood Duty Officer responds quickly. "Dispatch sub-hunter aircraft to the Atlantic Coast of Ireland, vicinity of Bundoran, to track SSBN *Vengeance* and report. Order the SSN Turbulent to locate and follow the *Vengeance*, last reported off the Irish coast near Bundoran, and report."

Friday morning, 11:00 GMT

The *Domino* is now nearly stationary, well off Penzance. Crew are gathered in the mess. Prim is with them. A voice on the sub's intercom says, "stand by for BBC news." The news anchor's voice is patched through:

Here is the news. Our top story continues to be the nuclear missile submarine, SSBN *Vengeance*, commandeered by her officers and crew and re-christened the *Domino*. The Prime Minister has been meeting with the Cabinet to discuss the challenge that the *Domino* affair poses in terms of both nuclear weapons command and control, and the larger question raised by the officers and crew: Does Britain need nuclear weapons? In a surprising development, a bill was just introduced to Parliament that would, if passed, commit the British government to verifiable nuclear disarmament within six months.

The crew applauds and cheers.

For more on that story, let's hear from our correspondent at Parliament, Lydia Fallon.

"The bill approved at the Cabinet meeting this morning for submission to Parliament would commit the UK to disassembling all its nuclear weapons in the next two months, thereby rendering them inoperable. In phase two, the radioactive cores of the UK's arsenal would be reprocessed over the following four months for use as nuclear fuel under the supervision of the IAEA. Parliamentary debate is scheduled to begin Monday morning at 9 AM."

"Already MPs have been inundated with calls to support the officers and crew of the *Domino* and to follow through with British nuclear disarmament. A large and peaceful street demonstration in favor of nuclear-weapons divestiture is now in full swing outside the Houses of Parliament. It is expected to swell to ten thousand or more people this afternoon, bringing traffic to a halt in Central London. Rumors are circulating on the Internet and in the media of an even larger, nationwide strike for world nuclear disarmament tomorrow. For the BBC, this is Lydia Fallon reporting from Parliament."

The crew rises, claps, and cheers.

Thank you, Lydia. Demonstrations in the UK that could bring the country to a virtual standstill on Saturday are being planned by numerous peace groups, joined by sympathizers whose enthusiasm for a world free of nuclear weapons has been boosted by the action of the crew of the *Vengeance*... or the *Domino*. The British-based Campaign for Nuclear Disarmament, the CND, is promoting a nationwide Day of Solidarity with the crew of that sub tomorrow, Saturday, and they plan to continue every Saturday until the British government commits itself to verifiable nuclear disarmament. This Saturday is being called "D-Day, *Domino* Day" by the organizers. The CND statement refers to the actions of the "courageous crew of the *Domino*" as being "a clarion call to the world to turn back the doomsday clock." The CND is calling on all nuclear-weapons states to join the UK in ridding the planet of nuclear weapons once and for all.

There are more cheers and applause from the crew.

Abolition 2000 and its affiliates are calling for worldwide observance of a rolling candlelight vigil this coming Sunday, at 7 pm local time in every time zone, starting with New Zealand and ending with Hawaii. The General Secretary of the World Council of Churches has called on all member churches to ring their bells for seven minutes this Sunday evening, and on successive candlelight vigil Sundays, at 7 pm local time, to express solidarity with those who are witnessing for nuclear disarmament.

Again, the crew erupts with cheers.

For reaction now from the European Union, we turn to France, the only other nuclear power in the EU. Our correspondent Nigel Langlois filed this report earlier today.

"French reaction to the events taking place aboard the *Vengeance*—or *Domino*—has been mild so far, largely because France has invested heavily in her own nuclear industries, in particular nuclear-fueled power plants. However a group named the

ACDN, *l'Action des Citoyens pour le Désarmement Nucléaire*, has called for gatherings in town squares throughout France on Sunday evening at 7:00, as part of the worldwide rolling candlelight vigil.

"There is also talk here of organizing 'D-Day' flotillas of private boats all along the coast of France, tomorrow, Saturday, at noon. They would be carrying *Domino* sympathizers hoping for a chance to welcome and applaud the submarine's crew. These flotillas should be especially in evidence off the coast of Normandy, with its 'D-Day' associations. Participants are sending invitations on marine radio to the *Domino* and its crew to surface and join them. They hope to spot the *Domino* and to provide human shielding for her if she surfaces in Normandy, or indeed anywhere in French waters."

"French policymakers are said to be monitoring closely the popularity of these demonstrations, as they consider the future of their own nuclear weapons program, their so-called *force de frappe*, which, like the UK's, includes four nuclear missile submarines. One or two of them are always on patrol and ready to launch their deadly payloads at a moment's notice."

The radio signal starts to fade out.

"Reporting from Paris, this is Nigel Langlois . . ."

There is more applause from the crew, who then resume their animated conversations in small groups, happy that the world is responding to their actions.

Drawing down its floating antenna, the *Domino* now dives deeper and begins a slow course toward its intended Saturday rendezvous off the coast of Brittany.

Friday night, 23:30 GMT

As midnight approaches, the alarm on the display at Northwood starts flashing again. It all seems like a repeat of the previous evening, but with the mobile phone location being tracked to the central west coast of Ireland, in Galway Bay.

The Duty Officer again reacts as before. "Dispatch sub-hunter aircraft to the Atlantic Coast of Ireland, vicinity of Galway Bay, to track the SSBN *Vengeance* and report. Order the SSN Turbulent to locate and track the SSBN *Vengeance* along the Irish coast near Galway, and report."

Saturday morning, 08:30 GMT

After a hasty breakfast, Leslie identifies a crew member, Tim, with some experience operating a video camera. He agrees to assist Leslie with her interviews. Her plan is to talk next with the two missile launch officers aboard the submarine.

She begins in her usual manner. "I am speaking to you from a ward room aboard the *Domino*, as the Trident nuclear missile submarine *Vengeance* has been renamed by its crew. It is early Saturday morning, and the sub is running deep and quiet in the direction of Belle-Isle, off the coast of France in Brittany. That is where a second planned surfacing and demonstration is expected to occur today, Saturday, at noon French time, which is eleven hundred GMT. The crew of 120 or so aboard this sub have been listening with great interest to news reports of world reaction to their peace and disarmament actions. They are cheering the news that public and even political responses to their 'taking the sub off line' have been so favourable.

My guests for this interview are the submarine's two missile launch officers, Julian Strobin on my right and Elliot Pisk on my left. Each officer, standing at separate consoles, would have to agree that an order to launch was authentic, and both would have to turn their keys simultaneously to effect any missile launch. Julian, may I ask you first, and then Elliot, where you're from in the UK? Is there a long tradition of military service in your families?"

Julian replies, "I'm from Leicester, in the midlands, and there is no particular military history in my family. My father is an account-ant and my mother teaches school."

Pisk responds, "I'm from West London. I rarely even saw the ocean before I enlisted. My father served in the Korean war, but hardly ever talks about it."

Prim then inquires further. "Were you given psychological screening when you applied for this job? Julian?"

"Are you kidding?—batteries of tests and interviews, and only after serving on other subs in less demanding roles were we promoted to this Vanguard-class missile sub's crew, and then to launch officer positions."

Pisk nods his agreement.

Prim continues. "Your positions would seem to require extreme reliability, an absolute and uncompromising sense of duty, and the peculiar ability to obey orders without worrying much about the human consequences. May I ask what accounts for your change of heart? For your having gone against your training, even against your own stable personalities, as it were? Elliot?"

"I still have a lot of respect for authority," says Pisk. "It's just a matter of whose. When I got involved in deep discussions with other crew members and officers about what we *would* or *would not* do if real launch orders came, I listened to our skipper in particular. Duff McGinty being about as dispassionate and clear-headed a man as you'll find, I was inclined to respect his reasoning. He said that the matter of obeying immoral and illegal orders, and then potentially being judged a war criminal, must not be taken lightly. It was no defense at Nuremberg. Why would we expect it to work for us today?"

After a pause to let the weight of his rhetorical question register, Elliot continues. "Realistically, one can't just blindly obey nuclear retaliation orders, incinerate half the world, spread radiation poisoning over the whole planet, and expect to be held unaccountable because one was 'just obeying orders.' We have been put in an impossible position: to be willing to become mass murderers on behalf of a country that doesn't even have the death penalty any more. Does that make sense?"

With a nod of comprehension to Eliot, Leslie turns to the other missile launch officer. "And how did you come to your change of mind or heart, Julian Strobin?"

"In terms of my personality, I think you'd be right in calling me a science and math geek. A left-brained kind of guy—all head, no heart ... until now. For me, launching ballistic missiles from underwater was pretty much an intriguing engineering problem. What caused a conversion in my case, I think, was becoming aware of my heart finally kicking in. I had been a 'head' guy for years. Look where it's landed me! I rose—*sank* may be a better term—to become one of the best-paid, most stable, on-demand mass murderers on the planet. I became a trigger-puller, an executioner, ready to exterminate hundreds of thousands of innocent non-combatants—ordinary people with children and extended families just like we have in Britain. When listening to Chaplain Matthew's reflections, and witnessing his blessing of the photographs, something stirred inside me, calling me to say, 'Whoa! Wait a minute!' While I'm not religious, I understand the sanctity of life. I saw no reason *not* to listen, *not* to pay attention to what Denis was saying."

Probing deeper, Prim asks, "How do you feel right now about the potential consequences of your dissent? Surely you both realize that you could be court-martialed and imprisoned for many years for what you are doing."

"At first," replies Pisk, "I used my head to work the odds, and gave us a 50-50 chance of coming out of this disobedience action as folk heroes, regardless of how the Royal Navy finally treated us. Since listening to the news, I think our odds of being greeted as the new Robin Hoods, who saved not only Sherwood Forest, but the entire northern hemisphere, maybe the whole planet, are likely to be 80-20 in our favor. I really believe the world is behind us now. I only hope that the Government will agree with us and, even if we're found technically guilty of dereliction of duty at some later date, we might be granted pardon by the Queen or King."

Strobin adds, "It didn't take me long to realize, once we decided to face the genocide issue squarely, that the well-being of the whole human family and our beautiful planet were far more important than my particular paycheck... I also knew that there is strength in numbers. We could hold the moral high ground if we worked together on this 'call to sanity,' this 'request to disarm.' I fully expect several neutral countries to grant us sanctuary if it comes to that. So I'm feeling good about this. I think I'm right where I belong, strange as it sounds. I'm comfortable being deep beneath the ocean and on moral high ground."

Prim then asks, "What kind of reception do you anticipate off the coast of France?"

Pisk's eyes light up. "It could be great fun! We do have a couple of crew members who are fluent in French, so we won't have any trouble communicating. Some members of our missile-launch crew are thinking of staging a symbolic action to show clearly how serious our intention is never to launch these missiles." Looking at Strobin, he asks, "Shall we keep it a surprise, Julian, or let her in on it?"

Strobin reflects for a moment, then replies. "Well there's probably no need to keep it quiet, since this report won't get aired until after our stunt is over."

Turning to Prim, he explains, "We're hoping to weld our missile hatches shut on the afterdeck, while the cameras roll. We think people need to see us doing this in order to be convinced of our sincerity. And while most of us don't speak French, we're pretty sure that our message to our counterparts in the French Navy will be well understood. For the sake of European solidarity, as well as the good of humanity, we need the French to join us in ridding Europe of nuclear arms."

"Thank you both. Reporting from aboard the *Domino*, this is Leslie Prim for BBC television news."

CHAPTER 6

UNE COMÉDIE FRANÇAISE

The French in their "bateaux" await
With Veuve Cliquot a nautical date.
"Vive le Domino" cheers,
Reverberate in their ears,
"Venez vite!" more "théâtre" to create!

Saturday morning, 11:00 GMT.

The *Domino* is now exactly five kilometers southeast of Belle-Isle, submerged some ten meters. It's Saturday at 12:00 noon local time. Fifty or more small craft of all kinds are forming themselves into a ring-shaped flotilla around prearranged GPS coordinates. Many carry signs with slogans like "Vive le *Domino*," and "À bas les bombes nucléaires," and "OUI au désarmement," and "Sanctuaire à l'équipage du *Domino*."

We hear shouts in French as the conning tower of the sub breaks the ocean's surface in the center of the flotilla. The French hosts can be heard excitedly shouting "Le voilà!" "Ah, je le vois!" "Regardez! C'est le *Domino*!" "Vive le *Domino*!" The small craft draw nearer to the sub, tightening the circle.

The crew hastens onto the deck. Some sailors affix the name *Domino* to both sides of the "sail"—the conning tower. Prim and her substitute cameraman, Tim, quickly get set up atop the tower and start video recording. Several French video cameras are capturing the scene from nearby boats, as well.

One of the French skiffs in the entourage—an inflatable, with a Frenchman waving and holding up a big bottle of *Veuve Cliquot* Champagne—makes a beeline for the sub, skidding to a halt on the latter's rounded flank. The Frenchman with the Champagne bottle reaches forward, speaking in a heavily Gallic accent. "Zees is a gift from ze people of France to ze officers of ze *Domino*. Please! Take eet! You need eet to re-baptize your *sous-marin* properly."

Crew from the sub take the champagne, bow to the courier with shouts of *merci*, and ease his boat back into the water. By now, McGinty has emerged in full-dress uniform, holding a placard saying *Le 'Domino.'* He has the crewman bring the Champagne bottle to near the front of the sub, where he proclaims, with one arm raised in benediction while he holds a sign up with the other hand: "I hereby rechristen you... the *Domino*!"

He nods to the crewman, who smashes the bottle against the steel hull. Applause and cheers erupt on deck, and horns sound from the surrounding flotilla.

McGinty walks back toward the conning tower, smiling, waving, and blowing kisses to the French flotilla. Tim, the cameraman, is recording the whole ceremony on video.

Still on the conning tower, Leslie soon takes her place in front of the camera and begins her narrative. "This is Leslie Prim reporting from the conning tower of the SSBN *Domino* at noon French time on D-Day, or *Domino Day*, as this Saturday is being called. We are just off the coast of Brittany, a couple of kilometers east of Belle-Isle, where we have been surrounded by a flotilla of enthusiastic French citizens in boats of all shapes and sizes. We can hear shouts of "Vive le *Domino*!" in the background. One of our French-speaking crew is about to address the flotilla. Let's see what he has to say."

The camera refocuses on James, a French-speaking ensign. He is standing with McGinty to his right, using a hand-held bullhorn.

"Salut, citoyens français! Au nom de l'Équipage du Domino et du Commandant McGinty, à ma droite, nous vous remercions de votre encouragement, et de votre désir pour le désarmement nucléaire total."

[Greetings, citizens of France. We thank you, in the name of the crew of the *Domino* and of Cmdr. McGinty, on my right, for your support, and your desire for total nuclear disarmament.]

Applause is heard, and small-boat horns are sounded in approval. A French TV reporter can be clearly seen on one of the nearby boats, describing and video-recording the event. Two teams of sailors on the rear deck begin to position themselves with acetylene torches above the missile hatches closest to the tower.

James continues, *"Nous voudrions vous offrir une preuve concrète de nos intentions. Vous verrez devant vous des membres de l'équipage avec des postes de soudure pour fermer les panneaux de nos missiles, afin qu'ils ne puissent jamais s'ouvrir. Nous fermons ces panneaux à jamais au nom de toutes les créatures de la terre, surtout au nom des hommes, des femmes, et des enfants de la famille humaine."*

[We want to give you a demonstration of our intentions. You will see before you some crew members with welding equipment. They will use it to seal the hatches of our missile tubes, so that they will never be able to be opened. We are sealing these hatches shut in the name of all living things on earth, especially in the name of the men, women, and children of the human family.]

James continues with his masterful French oratory, whipping up the crowd's enthusiasm by using some well-honed rhetorical devices, like these calls and responses:

"Vive l'humanité!"
The French shout *"Vive l'humanité!"* in reply.

61

"*Vive l'Angleterre!*"
The French shout "*Vive l'Angleterre!*"

"*Vive la France!*"
They echo "*Vive la France*," accompanied with horns and bells.

"*Vive la paix!*"
They shout "*Vive la paix!*"

"*Encore, Vive la paix!*"
They cry "*Vive la paix!*" louder.

"*Encore, Vive la paix!*"
They cry "*Vive la paix*" still louder.

He give a thumbs-up, and small-boat horns again blast their approval, with applause and much clamor in the background. Then he points to the rear deck.

The video-cameras aboard boats of the flotilla now focus on the rear deck of the *Domino*. Leslie, looking down on the proceedings from the tower with the camera held above and behind her, comments in a somewhat hushed voice: "As you can see, crew members are using acetylene torches to weld the hatches of this Trident sub's missile tubes shut, effectively making any future launches of these missiles impossible."

The work of welding goes on in relative silence, but with applause each time one of the welding teams, of which there are two working in parallel, leaves one hatch and moves on to the next.

Still on the sub's tower, Prim turns and approaches McGinty, who has been scanning the horizon with binoculars. Tim is following her with the video camera.

"Commander McGinty, would you like to comment on what we are witnessing on the afterdeck?"

Turning to the camera, with binoculars in hand, McGinty replies, "What you are seeing, ladies and gentlemen, is pretty self-explanatory. It's a form of free speech that goes beyond words. It's something that everyone can understand—like what happened in Berlin in 1989, when the people started dismantling the wall. History and humanity were on the side of the dismantlers, and the politicians were wise enough to 'get it.' They let it happen, and they even managed to do what the people couldn't do, which was to work out the legal and financial details."

Leslie then asks, "Do you think the French will follow suit?"

"We certainly hope that our government—but also the government of France—will work out the details of a nuclear-weapons-free zone in Europe soon. If that happens, I think the other nuclear-weapon states will follow our lead, because the world is *ready* for this. When the US sees that it no longer faces any nuclear threat, I'll wager the American people will insist on rejoining the world community through nuclear disarmament, too."

McGinty turns, and again lifts his binoculars toward the horizon. He seems nervous. He murmurs, "Uh oh."

Just then, over the conning tower annunciator, they hear the message, "Sir, British destroyer spotted on radar bearing 220 degrees."

"Roger—I've got a visual," replies McGinty. "She's approaching at flank speed. Recall the crew and prepare to dive."

A dive alarm sounds on deck. As the crew hurries back inside and closes the hatches, a French military helicopter appears in the distance, closing quickly.

"Are you going to have to take evasive measures, Captain?" asks Prim.

"The Admiralty has been sending us messages claiming that they are not planning to attack us, but will wait us out instead. So I imagine that the French chopper will do no more than observe and report. The Royal Navy would still like to track us, I believe, but we don't need that... Too bad our little welding party is being interrupted. We'll have to finish the job later."

Turning to James, the French-speaking sailor, McGinty asks,

"James, would you quickly uses your bullhorn to ask the French flotilla to escort us out to sea? See if you can get them to run interference with the destroyer for a while after we dive. We'll need their engine noises to cover our escape." James uses his bull-horn to relay this request to the French flotilla, and they wave in understanding and agreement.

As the waves start to wash over the deck of the *Domino*, Prim, still on the tower with Tim and James, turns quickly to the camera and says, "Aboard the *Domino*, which is starting to dive and take evasive action off the coast of France, this is Leslie Prim reporting for BBC Television News."

As the *Domino* slips beneath the waves, with a French military helicopter now hovering overhead, the French citizens' flotilla continues to escort the disappearing sub toward open water to the south. Ample footage of the whole episode is being recorded for RTF, the French TV network. Some speedboats in the flotilla race ahead to buzz and harass the oncoming British destroyer.

Saturday morning, 11:40 GMT.

With the *Domino* now completely submerged, McGinty and Hartwell are at the bridge planning evasive action. Prim, to one side, looks on. Hartwell remarks, "We can outrun that destroyer, but he'll be directing planes. How can we throw them all off our tail?"

McGinty replies, "For now, energize a decoy torpedo that sounds like us and launch it due south at a depth of 100 meters, programmed to weave if pinged. We'll see if they take the bait. Launch when ready."

Hartwell relays some orders to the torpedo room, through an intercom. After a minute, he reports back to the Skipper, "Decoy torpedo away, sir."

"Good!" Turning to the helmsman, he orders the *Domino's* propulsion cut to dead slow, as she hovers near the ocean's floor.

"Let's sit tight and quiet for now. We haven't got far to go to reach Falmouth this evening, and I'll bet our French friends are creating enough confusion overhead to cover nicely for us, for the time being... There are some container ships running northwest along the coast. In about an hour we'll see if we can slip out, line up beneath one, and shadow it up to the channel."

CHAPTER 7

A CABINET OF SURPRISES

The cat that is chasing the mice,
May be hungry, or naughty, or nice.
At times, when her aim
Is prolonging the game,
That cat may begin to think twice!

Saturday, 12:00 noon GMT

Back in central London, on Downing Street, near the Prime Minister's residence, a crowd has again formed with signs and banners demanding nuclear disarmament. Some are beating on noisemakers, as others rhythmically chant:

"*Domino, Domino*, no more Nukes!"
"*Domino, Domino*, no more Nukes!"

Inside the Prime Minister's residence, Madam PM is seated in her office. She is watching Headline News from the USA.

Good morning, it is 7:00 a.m. here in New York, on an overcast Saturday morning. Our top story continues to be a commandeered British nuclear missile submarine, the *Vengeance*, now called the *Domino* by its crew. It surfaced about an hour ago off the coast of Brittany, in France, near the island of Belle-Ile. Sources tell CNN that it was quickly surrounded by a flotilla of supportive French pleasure craft, one of which offered the British crew a bottle of Champagne with which to officially rechristen the sub the *Domino*.

After the brief renaming ceremony, the crew began welding shut the hatches of its sixteen Trident missile tubes, in a demonstration of the seriousness of their disarmament intentions. The French entourage cheered and sounded their horns as this operation proceeded. The crew were about half way through the job when a British destroyer, approaching in the distance, forced the sub to dive and take evasive action. Some video of this episode, shot by a French camera crew, should be available later this morning.

Meanwhile, in London, massive demonstrations in support of nuclear disarmament have begun to take shape. Organizers are calling today "*Domino* Day," or D-Day, and they are focusing on the Houses of Parliament, where they hope that a bill introduced last Friday by the Government, calling for British nuclear disarmament within a matter of six months, will be quickly passed. The parliamentary debate on the proposal is scheduled to begin Monday.

An intercom buzzes, the PM mutes the telly, and a secretary's voice is heard: "The Cabinet has assembled and is awaiting your arrival, Madam."

"Coming right away." She starts down the hall.

Everyone stands as the Prime Minister enters, and she motions them to sit down. Present are the same Ministers as in the previous cabinet meeting, along with Strong, the Secretary of State for Defence, and his entourage of high-level naval officers.

The PM opens the meeting with, "Well, ladies and gentlemen, news of the *Domino*'s surfacing in France an hour ago, and the action by the crew to weld her missile hatches shut, has already gone all 'round the world. I just got it from Headline News in New York. I must admit—Commander McGinty and his crew are staging a brilliant series of symbolic acts."

Turning to Strong, she asks, "What's the view from the defence sector, Marshall?"

"The *Vengeance* is playing a very skillful cat-and-mouse game with us, Madam Prime Minister. Three days ago, McGinty evidently slipped someone ashore on the west coast of Ireland with several of the crew's personal mobile phones, because for each of the last three nights MI5 has picked up brief calls from one or another of them at around midnight, but at widely different Irish coastal locations. And of course we scrambled our planes and submarines to scour the seas around each site, but to no avail."

The PM continues, "The news media are reporting that the sub was pursued not more than an hour ago by one of our destroyers. What's the latest on that?"

Strong motions to Hodgson to answer. "Our French Navy colleagues had gotten wind of the possibility of a 'D-Day' surfacing of the *Vengeance* along their coast at some time today. They were patrolling mainly Normandy looking for her. Apparently some disinformation was circulated on the Internet suggesting that Normandy was the shore to watch, with its D-Day associations. Shortly after the sub surfaced further south, off Brittany, the French Navy radioed to us where she was. We sent the HMS Kent, which was on patrol just off Finistère, to track her. McGinty obviously spotted the frigate coming and took evasive action."

"And did the sub escape?"

"She seems to have sent a decoy torpedo on a beeline south, toward Spain, and the Kent took the bait. Other ships and planes in the area are now being sent to widen the search, but there's a lot of shipping along that coast. We've lost her for now."

Thoughtfully the PM then asks, "Aside from the drama of the chase for its own sake, what's the point of continuing to pursue the

Vengeance? I mean, with our nuclear disarmament bill likely to garner strong support in Parliament, might this tactic be counter-productive? Or worse, hazardous?"

Nods of assent and murmurs of "Here, here!" are heard around the table.

The PM continues. "Couldn't we end this charade more quickly if we simply transmitted an amnesty to the *Domino*'s crew and officers? We certainly would not want to kill the goose that— surprising as it may seem—is laying for us a golden egg of potentially enormous political and financial value."

Rakewell jumps in, trying to deflect policy speculation and redirect the conversation to the military issues. "Might amnesty be a bit premature, Madam? No charges have been filed yet, let alone a court martial convened."

Noises from the street are becoming more audible; the PM excuses herself, walks over to a window, and looks out on the demonstration.

Signs are waving, and street theatre characters wearing domino-style vests are acting out anti-nuclear skits even more outrageous than before. She returns to the large rectangular table where the cabinet meeting is in progress. Members are murmuring quietly to one another.

"Very well," she says. "There seem to be varying opinions at this table regarding the merits of pursuit vs. amnesty for the officers and crew of the *Domino*. Ladies and gentlemen, an open question: Shall we drop the stick and offer the carrot? Seriously, shall we call off the pursuit of the *Domino* and offer the crew amnesty? Just to try to bring an end to these capers?"

Tom, the UN Ambassador, raises his hand.

"Madam Prime Minister, let me suggest that there is probably broad sympathy among the Cabinet as a whole, if not necessarily among our guests from the Royal Navy, for forbearance with respect to this crew's action. Theirs is not a simple hijacking. It is a form of ethically significant political speech... from sane, credible British citizens with real moral courage. It could well be argued that the crew are dissenting 'out of necessity'... and so are fully in compliance with international law. Then there's the popularity issue. Let's be honest. These men are already international folk heroes. Judging from reactions in the world press, they have taken the world by storm. They are poised to become exceptional roving ambassadors of good will for the UK. I haven't seen anything like it since... since the Beatles!"

Laughter erupts around the table. Heads nod in agreement.

The PM asks for a show of hands. "Shall we call off pursuit of the *Domino*?"

All hands go up except those of Strong, Rakewell, and Hodgson—the military contingent, who would abstain from showing their political sympathies in any event.

"Thank you," says the PM, who then turns slowly to Strong.

"I'm honestly afraid that if we pursue that sub too doggedly, Marshall, we might cause an accident that we would all regret. The last thing we need is to cause a collision while in hot pursuit of the sub, with loss of life and materiel, and very possibly a catastrophic release of radiation. It seems clear that this government must roll back serious pursuit of the *Domino*, and insist that the Yanks stay far clear of her."

Applause arises from all around the table. "Here, here!"

"So how shall we handle this?" the PM asks again. "Shall we send the *Domino* a message informing them that... let me think...

(a) Active pursuit of the *Domino* has been suspended,

(b) No attempt will be made to disable the sub, and

(c) No charges will be filed against the crew or officers, provided that no irreparable damage is done to the sub. Do these points sound reasonable?"

Murmurs of approval are heard, as heads nod in agreement.

Hodgson then asks, "What about getting the sub back? Can we set a deadline? They still have two months of provisions left, and could quickly change from 'roving ambassadors of good will' to loose cannons. They could circle the globe twice, staging their antics, if we did not give them a compelling reason to cease and desist."

The PM concedes. "Your point is well taken. Reactions?" She looks around the table.

The Foreign Secretary speaks up. "Taking a longer, strategic view, it could well be in our best interest to stimulate the broadest possible international dialogue on the subject of nuclear disarmament. We don't really want to be the only member of the club to disarm! I believe that it was no coincidence that the *Domino*'s skipper, McGinty, chose France for his second surfacing—or *epiphany,* to quote the sub's Chaplain."

He continues, with conviction. "If France follows our lead we will be on the way to a unified, nuclear-weapons-free E.U. within a year. Can you imagine? Can you just imagine what that would mean in terms of international good will toward Britain? And the value of Britain's moral stock? Why... it could usher in nothing less than a new world order, with the belligerent and strident United States government relegated kicking and screaming to the wings. How does *that* sound?"

Polite applause is heard all around the table.

The PM facetiously asks, "Do I sense a certain animus toward our great ally across the pond?" occasioning mild laughter.

"Seriously, though," she states, "nuclear weapons are an *American* invention of the 20th century. Who's to say we can't make nuclear disarmament a *British* invention of the 21st century?"

There are general murmurs of approval around the room, with "Here, here!" After calm returns the PM continues, addressing the Foreign Secretary. "What are you suggesting that we do vis-à-vis the *Domino* right now? Set a deadline for the sub to surrender?"

"Well... I think we have some choices. First, we could do as Admiral Hodgson suggests and offer an amnesty window, say, a week or ten days—hoping to have the Royal Navy reestablish command and control. But this might not be our wisest course of action in terms of the UK's long-term diplomatic or strategic objectives."

"Secondly, we could cut the *Domino* some slack by simply saying that we expect her to resume her quiet patrol at sea until the end of her scheduled deployment, and then return to base at Faslane. That way the ruckus would die down, we politicians would again reclaim the media limelight, and the *Domino*'s crew would be able to listen to the news and cheer from afar as our change of direction on nuclear deterrence unfolded."

"But as I'm talking, I'm coming up with yet a third option—namely for you, Madame Prime Minister, to speak directly with Commander McGinty on a secure, scrambled frequency, available at PJH Northwood. You could explain to him that we're not pursuing him anymore, and that amnesty is definitely in the works for him and his crew. You could also explain to him what our concerns are about getting other countries to follow the lead of the UK. It may be, for example, that McGinty, the skipper, and you, the Prime Minister, could collaborate secretly on staging a few more dramatic surfacings by the *Domino*, pursued by the Royal Navy more for show than anything else. The aim would be to cheer Robin Hood on ... to stimulate worldwide support for serious and total nuclear disarmament among the other nuclear-weapon states."

"Go on," says the PM.

"So... imagine arranging for another clandestine appearance of the *Domino* off the coast of France, this time perhaps in the Mediterranean, to further tip the scales of French sentiment in favor of the disarmament message. Another appearance could be off the coast of Israel. Then—forgive me if I get carried away—a parade by the *Domino* surrounded by small craft from every nation through the Suez canal. Next she could run right along the coasts of India and Pakistan, flying the biggest Union Jack and/or peace flag you've ever seen, to draw attention to the need for them to abandon their nuclear weapons, just as we have."

The PM is smiling to the point of purring. "Oooooo... this is getting good! What you're saying is that we need to consider maintaining the dramatic tension of a renegade sub, supposedly being pursued by a government that appears to be as befuddled as the Sheriff of Nottingham, as it attempts to rein in the bandits, because... because it is so *effective* theatrically, and in terms of media coverage."

The Foreign Minister responds, "Well, you have to admit, the world is currently being treated to a jolly good show: a dramatic cat-and-mouse game by us and our quarry. The world media are completely taken by it."

"Indeed!" says the PM. Approving murmurs are heard around the table.

"But let me suggest," the Foreign Minister adds, "that... just as real cats will sometimes toy with the mice they would otherwise eat, we should not rule out taking our time, too. In our case, the mice aboard the *Domino* have nuclear teeth—and they know how to roar. Let's not be too quick to stifle that roar!"

The PM and members of the Cabinet smile at one another as they look around the room. Heads quietly nod. It is clear that a high-level conspiracy is unfolding.

"Very well then!" she says. "We all have something to think about. Let's reconvene tomorrow, Monday, at 13:00 hours, when the debate will either be finished or in recess. I'm charging you all to the strictest secrecy. Not a word of this discussion will leak out."

Looking at Strong, she states bluntly, "Marshall, order the Royal Navy to cease pursuit of the *Domino* for the time being. Communicate with the sub a.s.a.p. Assure Commander McGinty that, while we may continue to make a show of looking for his sub, no efforts will be made to disable it. Let him know that I will be placing a direct and secure call to him at 0800 Monday morning."

Turning to the rest, she says, "I'll expect to see most of you in Parliament tomorrow at 0900 for the debate. That's it! Thank you for your attendance."

The meeting breaks up.

CHAPTER 8

LESLIE HEARS OTHER VOICES

Reporters, who stories pursue,
Know there's more than just one side or two,
Maybe three, maybe four,
Maybe five, maybe more.
Is there still time for this interview?

Sunday afternoon, 14:00 GMT

Back aboard the *Domino*, the Royal Navy pursuers of the previous day having apparently left the area, Prim and her new cameraman, Tim, are in her quarters reviewing the video just shot. Hartwell knocks and enters.

Prim looks up and smiles. "Oh, hi Richard! We were just reviewing the video shot yesterday. Pretty good stuff! Let me return to a spot where we can continue recording."

After touching some buttons, she looks up at Hartwell again.

"Tell me, Richard, has the *Domino* completely eluded the destroyer?"

He answers, "It seems that way. Late yesterday afternoon we slipped out into shipping lanes and positioned ourselves beneath a freighter moving slowly along the French coast toward the tip of

Brittany—Finistère."

"Will we make our evening rendezvous with Josh, my BBC cameraman?"

"Oh sure! We're already due south of Falmouth. Within a couple of hours we can be at the GPS coordinates where we will be able to surface and meet Josh after dark this evening. Not a problem."

Prim asks, "Then there's still time for me to do another interview, right?" Hartwell nods.

"I'm thinking of perhaps talking with a couple of crewmen in the enlisted ranks," she explains. "Men who might have a different slant on what's behind the crew's change of heart. Can you suggest some names? How about the one who speaks French—was it James?

"*Ah oui, mademoiselle.* He'd be good. Shall we stroll down to the mess hall and see if he's available or on duty? Just looking around down there, you never know whom else we might find."

They exit. Tim, staying behind, loads and adjusts the camera to record the next interview.

On the bridge, McGinty is studying a navigation display. The communications officer, Sparks, enters with a transcript in his hand.

"Sir, there's been a big change in the tune that Headquarters is singing. We have received a message issued by CINCFLEET himself saying that, in accordance with directives from the PM, this sub is no longer being pursued with intent to disable us. Here, read it."

He hands a message to McGinty.

"Thanks," says McGinty, and he starts reading softly. "No effort will be made to disable the *Vengeance*... He even writes that the political winds in the Cabinet have shifted in favor of both nuclear disarmament by the UK and amnesty for the officers and crew of the *Vengeance*... Well I'll be!... 'The Prime Minister will attempt to speak directly with Commander McGinty on Monday at 0800 on a secure, scrambled frequency.' How about that!"

Sparks adds, "They are asking us to acknowledge receipt of this message. Shall I?"

"It could be a trick," the skipper replies. "But I think it's worth the risk. Let's acknowledge it with the briefest acknowledgment and thank-you code in our book. Then we'll see if we attract any pursuers."

Turning to the helmsman, McGinty gives orders. "Take us to these coordinates, well away from shipping lanes, and bring her up to antenna depth. It could be fun to hear the coverage of the candlelight vigils this evening."

Sunday afternoon, 14:15 GMT

Prim has found her way to the mess hall of the *Domino*, where sailors are eating and relaxing. She chats casually with the off-duty sailors. Presently Hartwell enters with James, the French-speaking crewmember, so that he can be interviewed.

The intercom suddenly crackles to life, interrupting all conversations. It's the Skipper speaking. "Attention all hands: A dispatch has just been received from CINCFLEET that should be of interest. Admiral Hodgson states, in brief, that the *Vengeance* is no longer being pursued with intent to disable us. He adds, and I quote, that 'the political winds in the Cabinet have shifted in favor of unilateral nuclear disarmament by the UK and'—get this—'amnesty for the officers and crew of the *Vengeance*,' too."

There is an eruption of cheering and applause in the mess hall. McGinty continues over the intercom. "While this may be a trick to get us to return our submarine to Faslane, I still authorized a brief outgoing acknowledgment—a Thank You. The Royal Navy command now knows approximately where we are off the coast of France. We'll continue to monitor any tracking activity that might occur."

He adds, "You may also want to know that the Prime Minister asked to speak with me on a secure channel at 0800 tomorrow morning. I somehow don't think it's going to be an unfriendly call."

The crew applauds again, less robustly than before, probably because they really are not sure what the PM will be saying.

McGinty continues, "I'm hearing a more measured response to that last announcement. I really don't know what the ol' gal has in mind. She may just be jealous of Ms. Prim, and wanting to arrange a submarine joy ride herself!"

The crew laugh and applaud.

After a moment's pause, McGinty's voice comes back on. "More likely, if trust really can be established, the Prime Minister is going to need to figure out how to go forward from here with the best long-term interests of the UK and the world in mind. We may yet have a role to play in that scenario. We shall see. In any event, we should be approaching a point in another couple of hours where we can deploy our antenna and catch the news. The British unilateral nuclear disarmament bill gets debated tomorrow in Parliament. All in all, gentlemen—and lady, I'm feeling like we've had a successful week!"

The crew cheer and applaud, stomping their feet. One of them starts a song in honor of Prim:

For she's a jolly good fellow,
For she's a jolly good fellow,
For she's a jolly good fellow,
That nobody can deny . . .

When the singing dies down, McGinty comes back on the intercom: "Let me commend you all for your moral imagination, and your willingness to take a *big* risk for peace. I mean it... I am deeply proud of you all."

Again the crew cheer and applaud.

Sunday afternoon, 15:00 GMT

A short while later, Prim is setting up to interview two sailors in the corner of the mess hall: James, the French-speaking crewman, and Rohan, the British son of South-Asian parents, immigrants to the UK. They are seated on either side of her, and Tim has just given the sign that the video-recording has commenced.

"This is Leslie Prim reporting once again from the *Domino*, the Vanguard-class Trident nuclear missile submarine that has captured world attention. It is Sunday afternoon about 15:00 hours, and the sub is on its way back toward England after briefly surfacing in Brittany just off the island of Belle-Ile. As you may have seen on French TV, the crew welded about half the missile hatches on this sub shut, to considerable applause from the flotilla of French supporters. The crew members I'm about to interview are James, on my left, and Rohan, on my right. Let me start with you, James. As we saw earlier today, when you were speaking to the French citizens who greeted and surrounded us, you are virtually bilingual in French. How did this happen?"

James replies, "I was a 'diplomatic brat,' if you will. I went to a French lycée for my secondary schooling while my father worked at the British embassy in Paris, and I passed the French *bac* a few years ago."

"You seemed not to have any trouble speaking French loudly, even stirringly, as you did earlier today," Leslie observes. "Where did you pick up the ability to declaim in that language in such a confident manner?"

"It must have been drilled into me in school. We had to stand up in the lycée every week and recite from memory some passage or other from one of the French classic playwrights or poets. I'm afraid I'm better at quoting La Fontaine and Racine than I am at quoting Shakespeare."

"As a French-trained scholar, then," asks Prim, "what do you make of the events taking place aboard this sub?"

"Well, I see what we're doing as a *warning* to the world, in the broadest French sense of that word."

"Oh? How so?" asks Leslie.

"You know... the French don't have a simple word like our

'warn,'" James replies. "They either say *a-vertir*, which literally means 'to turn someone away,' like we might say 'divert' in English... or they say *pré-venir*, which means 'to come before,' or stand in front of someone... to get in their way."

"So your sense of what you and your shipmates are doing is, like, standing in the way of business as usual."

"Yes. In some strange way we Brits—this crew, at least—are giving the world a *warning* with a French twist: we're getting in their way, standing in front of the worldwide march to nuclear folly. We are holding up not just our hands, but our Vanguard-class nuclear submarine, directly in the path of that march, at right angles, and saying stop! Let's go in a different direction."

"Thank you, James. You've given us much to think about. Let me turn now to Rohan, a sailor of Indian descent, if I understand correctly."

Rohan, with his typical South-Asian inflections, replies, "Yes, Ma'am. My parents are both immigrants who grew up in Waltham-stow, married and raised a family there. That's not a very affluent place. I think the main reason I volunteered for the submarine service was to get ahead financially."

"So you enlisted for monetary reasons," says Prim.

"Yes, ma'am."

"May I ask what inspired you to be part of the revolt aboard this submarine?"

Looking uncomfortable, Rohan counters, "Is *revolt* the right word? It seems to me what we're doing is a highly principled action. It's not some kind of rowdy uprising."

"Sorry... let me rephrase the question. Why are you part of this 'highly principled action?'" asks Prim.

Rohan replies, after taking a moment to collect his thoughts. "Well I suppose you can guess that I'm not part of the white Anglican majority, either in the UK or aboard this vessel. I was raised a Hindu, but I honestly don't think the teachings of my religion were a factor in where I am now. As you know, we Indians, at least the educated among us, can claim as our own another prophetic figure—Mohandas Gandhi. He sincerely believed that the Indians and Pakistanis—the Hindus and Muslims—could and should co-exist. But when India, and then Pakistan, developed nuclear weapons, it seemed to lock them each in a permanent state of suspicion and mistrust. They need help from the whole world to back down. They won't be able to do it on their own. As James said, I want to stand in their way. I want to show them the road to real humanity. And you know... I'm not alone. We're not alone."

Prim then asks, "Are you saying that by participating in the nuclear disarmament demonstrations aboard the *Domino*, you want to send a message to your fellow Indians and Pakistanis?"

"Yes—that would be great... That's why it's so good to have a reporter like you aboard. Perhaps you'll help my fellow countrymen hear and understand this message. We Indians and our neighbors in Pakistan have no business developing and deploying weapons of mass-murder. The world has enough troubles without our having to inflict potentially endless suffering on our neighbors and ourselves. So I beg them to follow the example of the UK, if indeed the UK does what we hope it will do."

Prim continues, "You mentioned Gandhi. Did he say anything in particular to inspire you?"

"He always inspires me, may he rest in peace! You may have heard of Gandhi's seven deadly sins."

Prim nods, but doesn't say anything.

"One of them is 'science without humanity.' It describes very well what nuclear weapons represent. Our Indian nuclear scientists just did not get it! Homi J. Bhabha and Raja Ramanna, who 'fathered' India's nuclear program, were deaf to issues of humanity. So was Pakistan's nuclear weapons guru, A. Q. Khan. For all their intelligence, they were not very smart about what matters most. They must have been incapable of understanding the *sin* of science without humanity."

"You would not regard protecting one group of humanity from

genocidal attack by another group of humanity as a worthy goal? as something smart?"

Rohan replies, with a tone of disbelief, "Protecting? Yes. But this sub is not about protecting... It's only about retaliating. It can only offend; it can only multiply the disaster. It can't defend anything but itself—and that only by hiding."

"Were any of Gandhi's other seven deadly sins pertinent to your decision?"

He answers, "Gandhi also mentioned 'politics without principle.' Doesn't that describe the present world order? Look how the rich and powerful countries have set themselves apart. Even the UN has an elite club—the P5. And here I am, a British submariner, employed to maintain that dangerous and inherently unjust elitism."

Having had a background in international relations, Prim takes the cue. "You must be thinking of the nuclear-club bias built into the United Nations charter."

"Exactly!" Rohan replies. "The United States has been leading the victors of WWII along a path of nuclear elitism for more than seventy years, and look how much more dangerous the world has become. It has to stop!"

Getting more animated, Rohan adds, "I swear to you, every young Brit I've ever spoken with is disgusted at how much the UK has been imitating the US. We don't need a 'nuclear club' any more. The world is our lifeboat, after all! We don't want to blow nuclear holes in it!"

Visibly moved, Leslie pauses. Then she says, "Thank you both so much for your time, your reflections, and your convictions. For BBC Television, somewhere south of England, I'm Leslie Prim."

Sunday afternoon, 18:30 GMT

A few hours later, about half the crew are eating supper in the mess. The sub is motionless underwater, an antenna having been deployed to the surface to permit radio reception. The intercom comes alive when the radioman picks up a BBC News report. After the usual introductory music and beeps, the news anchor begins:

> At 18:30, our top story remains the surfacing at noon Saturday of the Trident nuclear missile submarine, SSBN *Vengeance*, renamed the *Domino* by her crew, in French waters off the coast of Brittany. French television reporters described a large and enthusiastic flotilla of pleasure craft surrounding the British sub as it surfaced. They cheered, blew horns, and even offered a bottle of Champagne to give the vessel a proper christening with its new name. It was an impromptu ceremony over which the skipper, Commander McGinty himself, presided.

The crew applaud and shout. Someone yells "Vive la France!"

> Then in a striking symbolic act, narrated by one of the sub's French-speaking crewmembers, two teams of sailors began welding the hatches of the Trident missile tubes permanently shut with acetylene torches. They got about half-way done when the Skipper ordered them inside and hastily put the sub into a dive, to evade a British frigate that was fast approaching in pursuit. The French flotilla of small boats reportedly ran interference for the sub so that it could make its getaway.

More shouting and foot stomping is heard from the mess hall.

> Elsewhere in the news, the worldwide rolling candlelight vigil in support of the Domino and of nuclear disarmament, announced for this evening, is well under way. It began in New Zealand many hours ago at 19:00 local time, and recently arrived on the continent of Europe after working its way through the time zones. Tens of thousands have assembled with candles in the streets of the world's major cities, from Wellington and Sydney to Tokyo—especially Hiroshima and Nagasaki—Beijing, New Delhi, Islamabad, Moscow,

Jerusalem, Rome, Paris, Madrid and the Scandinavian capitals. In virtually every city and town where church bells were present, they were rung for seven symbolic minutes starting at seven p.m.

The crew applauds.

Even the patriarchate of Moscow, which has long opposed any form of cooperation with Western churches, opted to join the bell ringing on this occasion. Somehow they got the bells in the churches inside the Kremlin itself to ring seven minutes at seven o'clock this evening. In the streets of Europe, many demonstrators are now wearing the domino motif as part of their personal attire: domino pins, shirts, earrings, and necklaces. Variations on the theme of toppling dominos are being acted out over and over again in popular street theatre, with competitions to see who can make the largest and longest topple. Let's hear now from our reporter in Paris, Nigel Langlois.

Church bells are heard in the background, as Nigel reports:

Good evening, Vince! Bon soir, everyone! Here in Paris, as it turned seven o'clock, the bells of Notre Dame Cathedral and seemingly every other church in this city started pealing in support of le désarmement nucléaire. Thousands upon thousands of French citizens were in the streets and open spaces holding candles. Some were singing a French version of "We shall overcome," that rallying cry from America's civil rights struggle, with the words (he sings) *Nous sur-mon-ter-ons*, or something like that, and "We will live in peace." I asked Madeleine, a serious-minded Parisian student carrying a placard that says "Oui au désarmement," what her true feelings were about the events of the past week. Let's listen.

In English, with a cute, sexy French accent, Madeleine replies into the microphone,

"We were astonished by the actions of the British sub, the *Domino*... and we really agree with them. We all want a nuclear-weapons-free Europe, and we can't have it without French cooperation. The era of De Gaulle is fini! We no longer need a French *force de frappe*. You know, France, like Britain, has four gigantic nuclear missile submarines. That is four *de trop*—how do you say?—four too many. All my friends are in favor of total elimination of French nuclear bombs, and everybody else's bombs."

Cheers and applause erupt from the crew. Some sailors bang dinnerware on the table, others shout "Go, Madeleine!" Langloi's report continues:

It's not just students marching in the streets of Paris this evening. There's a full spectrum of ages: parents with children, even the elderly. Many are wearing Domino-themed clothes and jewelry. Some have even applied face paint—squares of black with white dots, to their foreheads. I'm tempted to say Ash Wednesday is going to be preempted by Domino Sunday one of these days. I've never seen anything like it! Back to you, Vince!

Once again the crew is in an uproar, but they quickly quiet to be able to hear the continuing reportage.

Thank you, Nigel. Here in the UK, preparations for the seven o'clock candlelight vigil are well under way. Crowds are streaming into the centers of every city of any size, even small ones. In Brighton, where this all began, a long line of small boats is parading along the waterfront, sporting flags with Domino and peace motifs. In London, the crowd is already so large in front of Parliament, that there is no more room to squeeze anyone in. Signs are saying "Amnesty for the crew" and "No more nUKes" with the U and K capitalized. Groups are also chanting the now familiar refrain, "Domino, Domino, no more nukes!" There are even a few signs saying "PRO LIFE

= ANTI NUKE" as well, so this vigil seems to be drawing from all sides of the political spectrum. We'll continue updating you with live coverage as the evening progresses. The debate in parliament over nuclear disarmament will be carried live on BBC radio and television tomorrow morning, starting at nine o'clock.

The crew are giddy with excitement as applause and cheering resound through the submarine.

Sunday evening, 22:50 GMT

It is several hours later and night has fallen. Rendezvous time with Josh approaches. McGinty, Hartwell, and Prim are at the bridge.

The helmsman announces, "Sir, we're southeast of Falmouth at the coordinates you entered. Just rising to periscope depth."

McGinty calls for a sonar report.

"One small craft approaching off the starboard bow. Sounds like an outboard motor.

McGinty brings up the periscope and looks around. "I see the approaching vessel about 50 meters to our north. Let's surprise him! Up to drain the tower, do a radar sweep and report.

After a moment, another sailor's voice is heard: "Radar commencing... Radar showing nothing unusual, sir."

McGinty, momentarily turning away from the periscope, says, "It's a dark, overcast night. Just what we need! Take her up to the surface."

Turning to Hartwell and a group of sailors, he says, "Richard, you're clear for a rear deck exit." And to Leslie he asks, "Do you have the videos to give to Josh?"

"Yes," she says, holding up a sealed plastic bag, "Right here, Sir."

"Good! We'll be crawling along while you do the transfer."

The deck party exits. Turning to the helmsman, the skipper orders, "Ahead dead slow, bearing 280, and keep our deck above water."

"Aye-aye, sir. Ahead dead slow."

McGinty then turns to the duty officer on the bridge. "You've got command. I'm going to the top of the sail to make a mobile phone call to Chaplain Matthew on Iona. Let me know if anything naval approaches."

Atop the sail, McGinty dials the Iona Community. A familiar voice answering the phone surprises him.

"Iona Community switchboard. Good evening."

"Hi, Denis. It's me, Duff. We just surfaced to drop off some more video."

Denis replies "Wonderful! I've been waiting here at the switchboard for your call."

McGinty continues, "MI5 is probably monitoring us, so I won't give any secrets away. We were informed by CINCFLEET this afternoon that the hunt for the *Domino* has been scaled back. There's not going to be any effort to disable us, and amnesty will be granted to any crew involved in this exercise of conscience. They may be trying to entice us home soon. Have you heard a whisper of this in the media?"

"The part about no longer trying to disable you was mentioned, to avoid any risk of an accident, but nothing about amnesty for the crew. You must know that the *Domino* affair has been dominating the news all day, all weekend for that matter. And the rolling candlelight vigil is headed for America as we speak."

McGinty replies, "I was going to ask about that."

Matthew continues, "It's a huge story, Duff. I'm so proud of you and the men of the *Domino*. God knows we've been praying for a turnaround like this. You guys are like Jonah coming out of a whale in the 21st century. And Nineveh is listening, by God... they're *listening!*"

"Well there's more to come," quips McGinty. "More video with

Leslie's reportage and interviews. Now, about the pursuit, we'll know soon enough how seriously we are being tracked. And about the amnesty, I really don't know whether it's credible or not. How would you like to be our test case?"

Matthew answers, "Sure. I'm the perfect scapegoat if they want to arrest someone from the *Domino* and throw the book at 'im. Should I turn myself in to the military tomorrow?"

"Negative," says McGinty. I don't consider you AWOL, Denis. You're on special detail right now. Why don't you just go the nearest BBC-TV station tomorrow, if not in Oban then Glasgow, and offer your services as an expert commentator on the unfolding drama of the *Domino*? I'll test the Royal Navy's credibility by surfacing and phoning you every evening at 23:00 on your mobile phone—you still have it?"

"Yes, but I haven't dared turn it on yet for fear of giving my position away."

"OK," says the Captain. "Switch it on every evening at twenty-three hundred hours, and we'll hope to be in touch. By the way, the Prime Minister intends to speak directly with me tomorrow morning at 08:00 on a scrambler. I'll inform her that you are on special detail from our crew as a spokesperson. I'll tell her about your plans to be a BBC commentator. I'll remind her of the amnesty promise and ask that you not be arrested or otherwise interfered with by the Royal Navy or MI5. I'll recommend a temporary reassignment for you, Denis. Does this sound fair?"

Matthew replies, "Sure, it's fine. Talk to you tomorrow evening! By the way, tomorrow could be a landmark day, with most of the nation monitoring how Parliament handles the nuclear disarmament bill introduced earlier."

"Roger that!" says Denis. "Until later! Bye!"

After hanging up, McGinty looks over the edge of the conning tower. He sees Richard and Leslie, arm in arm, waving good-bye to Josh, who slowly motors away with the latest interviews on video.

Then McGinty calls down to them, over the edge of the tower. "If you two would like to wrap up in a blanket and take a few more minutes of privacy to breathe fresh air and admire the coastal lights, I think we can arrange that. No military aircraft or ships have been reported in the area. When the cat's away the mice can play!"

The couple smile up at him as he waves and disappears.

CHAPTER 9

THE CONVERSATION THAT NEVER HAPPENED

"Do keep up your disarming commotion,"
said the PM to those in the ocean.
"May the world take due note
How the men in your boat
Put a much-needed movement in motion."

Monday morning, 07:30 GMT

With the dawn of the new week, the *Domino* is submerged again, running quiet and deep in the English Channel. Sailors at breakfast are seen poring over the newspapers and magazines that Josh delivered, featuring front-page coverage of the *Domino* affair. Some hold up magazines with glossy cover stories, others point to coverage in German and French news magazines.

About a half hour later, at 07:59 GMT, Captain McGinty takes a seat at a console in the communications room. He is wearing a telephone headset. A computer monitor shows a secure, scrambled communication link being established. The Prime Minister's voice is suddenly audible:

"Commander McGinty, can you hear me?"

"Affirmative, Madam Prime Minister. Am I coming through?"

After about a two-second pause each way, presumably for descrambling, he hears, "Yes, thank you. I'm glad we can talk privately. I hope that you have not been pursued any more since yesterday afternoon's communiqué."

"We've had no sign of pursuit, Madam, and we have given our location away twice."

"Where are you now, Commander?"

"Deep in the channel, off Guernsey."

"Speaking person-to-person now—may I call you Duff?"

"Yes... please do!"

"Well, Duff, let's come right to the point—and I'll deny this if it ever comes out. I want you to know that the bold action that you and your crew have taken is very likely going to change the course of British history... and it couldn't have come at a better time."

McGinty pauses for a moment, then replies in a measured way. "Madam, I'm humbled by what you are saying. May I infer that your Government has not been unduly embarrassed by our nuclear disarmament action?"

"Initially it was enough to give us all apoplexy! But as my Cabinet began to consider what you were requesting, how you avoided any hint of extortion or blackmail, and how quickly your action garnered worldwide support, all the way from the Mayor of Hiroshima to the Pope, we really couldn't ignore what you were asking for."

She adds after a pause, "Everyone in my cabinet, with the exception of the Defence Minister, agrees that your words and actions are absolutely credible and deserve serious attention. The fact that you have made no threats, declared no deadlines, and not even issued any selfish demands, lifts this episode out of the realm of terrorism and hijacking altogether. In fact, I've instructed my government not to mention those hot-button words in any communiqués on the topic, although the American president is already beside himself with dire warnings of nuclear terrorism in the making."

"Very wise, Madam!" says the Captain. "We would not harm a hair on the head of any British subject, or indeed any human being. That's the whole point of our protest—to rid humanity of the threat of use of the dreadful payload of nuclear weapons we are carrying, and to inspire other governments to follow our lead."

The PM responds. "Your mention of other governments brings me to the real point of this call, Duff. And now I need you to clear the room you're in if others are watching or overhearing. This has to be for your ears only. Tell me when I'm safe to resume."

The Skipper looks around and finds no one eavesdropping. After a few seconds, he says to the PM, "The area around me is cleared, and I'm using a headset. I think you can speak confidentially."

"I believe that my government is going to win the debate in Parliament today. We may well have the approval of a draft unilateral disarmament bill in the House of Commons by this evening. It proposes two months to deactivate all our nuclear weapons, and another four months to dismantle them altogether and recover the cores for reprocessing as fuel. Some of my ministers don't want to see us go too far out on a limb and not be followed in our disarmament initiative."

"Yes... I understand."

"It has been suggested that the drama of your continuing evasion of the Royal Navy, and your roguish way of surfacing and rallying local flotillas whilst you carry out symbolic disarmament acts—all those theatrics should not stop too soon. It might be very useful in fanning the flames of support in other countries for what we'll very likely be doing in Britain. Do you get my drift?"

"Yes, Ma'am! I think we could stage a few more good shows for you. Especially with some land-based help in the background to contact the anti-nuclear groups in those countries and mobilize them as flotillas and rallies. Did you have any countries in mind?"

"Certainly France would be objective number one. If she disarms, it will be a real coup—the first time the E.U. has been nuclear weapons-free since the beginning of the cold war. It will give us the collective leverage we need, as Europeans, to lead a viable international coalition with real economic and moral clout as well as political credibility."

"I see," says McGinty.

"And so, quietly, and officially at arm's length, we would like the *Domino* to stage another—what does your Chaplain call it? Ah yes, another *epiphany*, once again in France, this time perhaps off the Mediterranean coast. Maybe you can weld a few more hatches shut, or conjure up some other dance routine."

McGinty replies, "Yes, I'm with you."

She continues, "We'll have the Royal Navy appear to track you and provide another cat-and-mouse show for the media. Of course, not a word of this scenario of ours must leak out. I would not let even your BBC reporter on board, Ms. Prim, know about our arrangement just yet. I trust you'll agree."

"Yes, of course, Madam. I'll be quiet, and hold up my end of the deal. I'll say only that you and I discussed amnesty scenarios and timing, and that we agreed to continue on our respective courses a bit longer. I'll acknowledge that we are visiting some other coastal locations, and engaging in more theatrics, to keep up the pressure. Can you warn the French forces off trying to track or disable us?"

"Yes. We'll advise them that it's not worth the risk of an accident, and warn them not to disturb the delicate negotiations we have going on, even as we give chase."

McGinty then asks, "And after France? Are you thinking... Israel? The way I am?"

"In fact, we are. We think you could pull off a whopper of a disarmament parade along the coast of Israel if you were escorted by an appropriately international flotilla. We wonder whether the I.A.E.A., if it got behind you, could round up some tall ships, a Greenpeace vessel, maybe even the Calypso. Symbolism counts in your kind of street—or should I say *fleet*—theatre."

"How would I or my crew arrange that, if our sub is still to all intents and purposes being pursued? If we're still on the lam?"

After a moment's reflection, the PM suggests, "Well... could you drop a trusted representative ashore to organize it directly with some prominent NGOs and peace groups? It has to look like a popular initiative—not a British government one."

"I've already got a key member of my crew ashore—our wonderful Chaplain, Denis Matthew, the one whose reflections probably did more than anything else to enable us to convert this sub from the *Vengeance* to the *Domino*. He's on his way to a BBC-TV studio in Glasgow today to see about offering expert commentary on the latest reportage from our sub. Those interviews should also be airing today, and I think they're going to get a lot of attention. He's our test case for amnesty, which was all but promised in a wire from Admiral Hodgson yesterday afternoon, evidently at your request. Can you please see that Matthew is not detained by MI5 or the Royal Navy?"

"Yes! I'll see to that. You may have your best intermediary right there. Shall I arrange to clue him in, or will you?"

McGinty replies, "Let me speak with him tonight, and I'll advise him that your office will be in touch about this. Will you send a trusted personal representative to Chaplain Matthew in Scotland to facilitate his contacts at the I.A.E.A. and other possible collaborators?"

"Yes, I can arrange that. So that's decided."

"Agreed," says McGinty.

"Now... after Israel, we're debating arranging for you and your flotilla to pass through the Suez canal and parade off the coasts of Pakistan and India, say, between Karachi and Mumbai. After that, you could return through the Suez into the Black Sea, and lead a floating peace demonstration along the coast of Russia."

McGinty replies, "We may need some Russian-language assistance, if and when we get that far."

"Consider it done. We'll have a fluent Russian speaker air-dropped to you."

"And after Russia, dare I ask? The east coast of the USA?"

The PM replies, "By that time, Duff, we may have a *real* parade—something official for you to lead. A disarming 'love letter' from Europe to the American people. Imagine our three other Vanguard missile launchers, plus the four French counterparts, all steaming down the east coast of the US, flags flying, flotilla following, toward that place in *Georgia* (she pronounces it '*Ge-o-gia*' with a southern US accent)... that place where you get your Trident missiles loaded and unloaded."

"King's Bay, *Ge-o-gia*, Ma'am," McGinty echoes in perfect imitation. "The Atlantic home port of the US boomer fleet—their Trident sub fleet."

By now the PM is chuckling softly. She then adds, "Well, I predict the nuke market is about to go from boom to bust. Do you think they'll take returns?"

McGinty replies, "We'll see, Ma'am... If they don't, we may just have to launch 'em back. One way or another, they'll have to deal with a few dissatisfied Trident nuclear submariners off their coast."

The PM continues, "And just wait till US public opinion gets mobilized. If they think we Brits are trouble, just wait until they hear from their own disarmament supporters. I'm already laying money on there being a march on Washington before June is over."

She chuckles. Then he chuckles, adding, "I imagine you're right."

The PM concludes, "Very well... I'll be back in touch on the scrambler when things become clearer. In the meanwhile, I'll have the Royal Navy act as if it is still chasing you, and we'll work out the details as we go."

"Thank you for your support, Madam, and good luck with the vote today."

They disconnect.

CHAPTER 10

THE REST OF THE STORY
(IN HEADLINES)

Front pages like these we'll not see
In our lifetimes, unless there can be,
A consensus that's for
No more nuclear war.
No more "vengeance" that comes from the sea.

With the conclusion of the secure phone call between Madam Prime Minister and Captain McGinty, a constructive—some might say creative—resolution of the tension between the British government and the "renegade" Trident missile submarine, the *Domino*, seems to have occurred.

What follows is a series of hypothetical headlines in major world newspapers that suggest how the disarming movement unleashed by the officers and crew—the "roaring mice"—of the *Domino* might play out in reality.

These headlines arbitrarily cover a number of months beginning with the date June 4, 2019, but any year in the first quarter of the 21st century would do. The dates are only used to suggest a relative timeline for how quickly the world might be carried along, once the nuclear disarmament wave—the first true *tsunami* for life—starts rolling.

The Times [London]
Tuesday, June 4, 2019

Parliament OKs
Nuclear Disarmament
PM Proposes Nuke-Free E.U.

**'Domino effect' credited with
popular vote**

The Times [London]
Sunday, June 9, 2019

Domino Crew Cheered
by French Flotilla
in St. Tropez, Cannes
Cirque du Soleil Performs on Deck

International New York Times,
Sunday, June 16, 2019

E. U. To Abandon Nukes
**French Government Joins
UK in Nuclear Disarmament Coalition**

The Times [London],
Sunday, June 30, 2019

Domino Flotilla Cheered Along
Israel's Coast, Tel Aviv to Haifa

Knesset to Debate Israel's
Nuclear Status

NOTE: On Israeli television that evening there was a report from the Wailing Wall and the Temple Mount in Jerusalem. Atop the Temple Mount, Muslims were seen leaning over and waving white handkerchiefs at Israelis gathered around the base of the Wall. Many Israelis waved back with white handkerchiefs and blew kisses.

Jerusalem Post,
Wednesday, July 3, 2019

Israel Opts for Nuclear
Weapons Elimination

Knesset advises PM to cooperate with the EU
to avoid trade embargos and diplomatic isolation

The Times of India,
Tuesday, July 23, 2019

India and Pakistan
Feeling the 'Domino' Effect

**Both Sides to Sign Non-Proliferation
Treaty and Eliminate Nuclear Weapons
Under UN Supervision**

**Indian Doctors for Peace and
Development Support Weapons Elimination**

The Times [London]
Tuesday, October 8, 2019

Domino Crew Awarded
Nobel Peace Prize

McGinty, Crew Share Honours

**Congrats Pour In From
Around the World**

The Moscow Times,
Monday, October 21, 2019

Russian Federation Joins
Nuclear Disarmament Coalition

Lucrative E.U. Trade Ties
Trump Military Agenda

The New York Times
Thursday, Nov. 7, 2019

WALKOUT AT U.N.

US REFUSAL TO JOIN NUCLEAR
DISARMAMENT COALITION
PROMPTS EXODUS OF DELEGATIONS
FROM UN HEADQUARTERS

World Community Presses US to Abandon Nuclear
Weapons or Face Trade Boycotts

International New York Times,
Wednesday, Nov. 20, 2019

UK Offers to Host the New U.N.

United Non-nuclear Nations (UN2) Charter Will
Turn the Tables on Remaining Nuclear-Armed States

International New York Times
Tuesday, March 17, 2020

US and China to Eliminate Nuclear Weapons Under UN2 Supervision

US President Yields to Public Pressure and Congressional Resolutions, Narrowly Avoiding Impeachment

UN2 Inspector Hans Blick to Direct Nuclear Weapons Disarmament Teams in China and USA. Rapid Compliance Predicted

CHAPTER 11

POSTSCRIPT FOR PEACE

If they bring back ol' Duff (déjà vu),
'Neath the flag of a new UN2,
He'll take youngsters to sea,
Dancing jigs on the lee,
He'll be mixing the old with the new.

A Sunny Day in May, Five Years Later

Several good years have passed. Once again Leslie Prim, the Orwell Prize-winning BBC reporter, finds herself walking along the Brighton esplanade. She is not alone.

Accompanied by her ex-Royal Navy husband, Richard Hartwell, she pushes a stroller with two small children. They soon reach a familiar *gelateria* at Grand Junction Rd., near where the story began. They proceed to order ice-cream cones. Just as Leslie is bringing hers to her lips, her mobile phone rings.

"Damn!" Groping in her purse with one hand, she mutters, "Who could that be?" She sees an unfamiliar number on the screen, but answers, "Prim here."

A familiar voice says, "Hello, Leslie?"

"Speaking... "

Aside, to Richard, she whispers, "I know this voice!"

"This is Duff McGinty," the caller continues, "who once phoned you from a Trident missile submarine that was badly misbehaving off the coast of Brighton. It was a few years ago. Remember?"

"Ah yes, I remember well! It was the sub that took the world by storm, stole my heart, and seems to have made the planet a much safer place to have babies again!" She looks at Richard, grins, and whispers, "It's Duff."

"Can I put you on the speaker phone, Duff?" she asks.

"Sure. Is Dick with you?"

"Yes, and so are the kids."

Richard chimes in, "Hi, Duff! What's up?"

Leslie adds, "We're walking along the waterfront again, right near where this whole saga started." Eyeing Dick suspiciously, she asks Duff, "Is this a setup?"

McGinty replies, "What a thought! By the way, can you see a long, low vessel out beyond the pier, with a big green UN2 flag flying?"

Prim squints toward the horizon, and exclaims "Yes, I can... Well I'll be! It looks like a sub... Dare I ask if you're on it, Duff?"

"In fact, I am. They dusted off the ol' Duffer to be the Skipper of a scientific expedition. It's a 'new wine in old wineskin' story, Leslie... The SSBN *Vengeance* has become the Oceanographic Research Vessel—the ORV—*Domino*, and we have a group of about thirty international students aboard. We're teaching them some new dance routines. Can you see them?"

Richard hands Leslie a surprisingly convenient pair of binoculars, to give her a better chance to observe the deck of the submarine. She glances knowingly at him, smiles, and raises the binoculars to her eyes.

"Just a second... Oh, Duff! What a marvelous sight! Those

students... they look so healthy and happy!"

McGinty's head is just barely visible atop the sail. He continues talking on his mobile phone. "Here's the scoop. We're heading tomorrow for the North Cape and the Arctic ice cap under UN2 auspices, to study global warming. We thought we'd stop at Newhaven harbour this evening and let the students have some R & R. Any chance I can catch up with you two for supper? I confess I'm already getting just a little tired of submarine food!"

"You're on, commander! And this time *you* come ashore instead of *me* going aboard!" counters Leslie.

They laugh, and Leslie and Richard wave from afar at the submarine and its dancers on deck, as they pass by. Occasionally a strain of familiar music—the Monty Python Flying Circus theme-song—reaches their ears. Some smaller vessels have gathered round the submarine to escort her to the harbour. The small flotilla fades in the distance, and the young family begins its walk home, stopping by some open markets for fresh produce and perhaps, just for old time's sake, a bottle of French champagne.

This particular bottle of *Veuve Cliquot* won't have to be sacrificed to a rechristening ceremony.

AFTERWORD

"Seriously, though, nuclear weapons are an *American* invention of the 20th century. Who's to say we can't make nuclear disarmament a *British* invention of the 21st century?" (p. 71)

ABOUT THE AUTHOR

T. F. Heck, a librarian/musicologist retired (as emeritus professor) from the Ohio State University, is a passionate peace advocate. He has authored several scholarly books on music and the performing arts, including *Commedia dell'arte: A Guide to the Primary and Secondary Literature*, and *Picturing Performance: the Iconography of the Performing Arts in Concept and Practice.* He believes that the arts have essential roles to play in furthering a culture of peace. The present hope-filled story exists as a screenplay, as an experimental theatrical script, and as the present work of fiction. Kindly contact the author with your responses via e-mail at **insights@aya.yale.edu.**

Made in the USA
Middletown, DE
19 June 2016